What the Statue Thinks
A Collection of Short Stories

MICHAEL GOODWIN HILTON

Wild Ink Publishing
LLC

Wild Ink Publishing LLC

A Wild Ink Publishing Original

Wild Ink Publishing

wild-ink-publishing.com

Paperback ISBN: 978-1-958531-40-2

Ebook ISBN: 978-1-958531-41-9

Any references to historical events, real people, or real places are used fictitiously. Names, characters, and places are products of the author's imagination.

For my family.

For Lawrence Sacharow,
who taught me that if it's in my imagination,
"it's valid."

CONTENTS

A HOLE IN THE WATER

B rady woke up knowing exactly what day it was, and he hated that he knew.

He turned on his phone. A text from Craig. "Ready to walk the sober mile old man?" Gentle ribbing with a hint of urgency.

Brady's birthday was a few days away. Thirty-eight, more than twenty years Craig's junior even though Craig insisted that Brady was much older "in spirit." There was something else behind the text, Brady could tell. An AA veteran's noble bid to head off a potentially triggering day ahead: the twenty-two-year anniversary of the death of Brady's father.

"There soon," Brady texted back then looked over at his wife, still asleep. He traced his fingers along the edge of her hip then tucked them beneath the waistband of her pajama bottom and scratched her backside. She grunted, reached behind, and batted him away.

"Stop," she protested, digging her face deeper into the pillow.

"I love you," he whispered into her ear.

She rolled to him and opened her eyes.

"You okay?"

"Why wouldn't I be?"

Stroking the side of his head. "Gonna meet with Craig?"

Brady nodded.

"That's good." She always felt better when he met with Craig, a custodian from the high school where Brady taught PE. More importantly, Brady's sponsor of almost three years.

His wife sat up and yawned dramatically then climbed out of bed. "Don't forget the steaks."

Brady tilted his head.

"I told you last night," she said. "Your birthday weekend!" She was determined to distract him as best she could from the seconds and minutes and hours ahead.

"Who's coming?"

"Sandy and Sean."

"Why?" he asked after a moment.

She gave him a look. "Just don't forget them okay."

"I have swim practice this afternoon."

"Store's open till six. Can you get there?"

"I'll get there."

They kissed, and Brady tried to drag her back down to the sheets, but she pulled herself away and headed for the shower.

Brady would join her shortly, but first, he needed to lay out his clothes. He opened the closet to retrieve his shirt, trying to avoid looking at the floor. Clothes in hand, Brady closed the doors. Moments later, he opened them again, bent down, and picked up the boots that had been tucked at the back corner as though begging to be forgotten.

When Brady pulled into Craig's driveway, Craig was raising his flags up the pole in front of his house. The Trump flag followed by the American flag. Craig turned and waved.

"Morning."

"Morning."

"Mind giving me a hand with the mulch before we head out?"

Brady checked his watch. "Think we have time?"

"Won't take long," Craig said. He led Brady to the backyard where bags of enriched soil were stacked against the shed. A white truck was parked close by, its doors hanging open.

"Got a second job?" Brady asked.

"Gus's shorthanded this time of year," Craig said, referring to the owner of a local florist. "He'll get more help once the kids are out of school for the summer. I try to help out with landscaping here and there. Do some deliveries. Doesn't hurt to have the extra money, especially for..." He trailed off.

"For?" Brady pursued.

Craig turned to him with a light smile. "Never know." He shrugged. "Things come up."

Craig bent and picked up a board from the floor of the truck and slid it along a pair of slots at the sides. He then added a second and a third, placing a pair of heavy clips at the ends to make a shelf. Brady noticed a line of red flowers in dark plastic pots behind the rear tires.

"Geraniums," Craig said. "Want one?"

"Hmm?" Brady grunted.

"Do you want a Geranium to take home to Karen?" Craig asked.

"How much?"

Craig hopped down, picked up one of the potted flowers, and handed it to him. "I'll spot you."

"You sure?"

"Let me show you something," Craig began. "You gotta pick out these brown dead petals here; see 'em?" Craig plucked out several shriveled specimens, moving his thumb and index delicately through the crown of red, surgically avoiding the healthy petals. "Called dead-heading," he explained. "Makes 'em look a lot nicer, doesn't it?" He patted Brady on the shoulder and climbed back into the truck. Brady put the pot back down and crossed to the shed to begin hauling over the mulch.

"Things are heavy," he commented.

"Rained yesterday," Craig replied. "Mulch soaks it right up. Consider it your morning workout."

"Already benched this morning," Brady said.

"I'll bet you did, arms like that. Set a good example for the kids."

Physically, Brady and Craig were almost nothing alike. Brady was medium height and brawny, while Craig was tall and lanky. Brady had short blonde hair, while Craig kept a long gray ponytail. Brady began his days with protein shakes, while Craig usually started with coffee and a couple of smokes on his side porch. But sobriety required a wide array of antidotes, both men knew, and nothing worked except what worked. Brady turned to inspect the pile of cigarette butts that usually teetered in the ashtray on the porch railing. He noticed several packed boxes stacked over each other beside the door.

"Going somewhere?" Brady asked, indicating the boxes.

Craig adamantly shook his head. "Just clearing out a few things from the basement," he said and quickly turned his attention back to the mulch bags.

Brady's eyes lingered at the porch a moment longer then shifted to the flagpole.

"Think he'll win?" Brady asked.

Craig followed his gaze then replied, his chest puffed, "Without question. You do too, right?"

"Hope so," Brady answered.

"Put your sign out?"

"Got it the other day," Brady said.

"But have you put it out yet?"

Brady shook his head.

"And why not?"

"Karen's still thinking about it."

"What's there to think about?" Craig asked, tilting his head slightly.

"She wants to watch the debates—?"

"The *debates*!" Craig yelled.

"Well, that's her, not me." Brady defended.

"Yeah, Mr. I-voted-for-Obama."

"Once," Brady clarified. "I voted for him once. Thought, what could be the harm—?"

"What could be the—?" Craig turned and punched one of the bags, splitting it open at the side. Loose dirt spilled out onto the floor of the truck. "Shit." He shook his head at the mess.

"Look, like I said, my mind's made up." Brady picked up a clod of dirt and tossed it toward the shed. "Women. Y'know."

Craig, staring off into the trees behind his property, spoke gravely. "For all our sakes, I hope everyone sees what's headed for us. I hope everyone sees what's coming. Gotta prepare ourselves. Mark my words. You do not want to be caught unprepared, trust me. Do not let your guard down for a second. When it comes for us..." He didn't finish the thought, as though doing so might conjure the unknown and the unthinkable.

Craig jumped down to the lawn and squeezed Brady's elbows. "Just looking out for you, brother," he said.

"I know."

"We gotta look out for each other and fight like hell for everything worth fighting for. Everything worth saving. Everything worth protecting. Am I right?"

Brady nodded.

"Still got time to walk?" Craig asked.

"Think so."

"Good. Let's hit it." Craig closed the doors of the truck. "Don't forget your Geranium."

Brady bent and picked the potted flower up off the grass. Minutes later, he tucked it underneath the passenger seat of his pickup, wedging it between the boots so that it wouldn't spill out onto the mat.

The sober mile wasn't really a mile, but that's how Craig always referred to the distance between his house and the beach where he once almost drowned. He had woken up one morning next to the bay wearing only his underwear, dripping wet and improbably alive. Later that same day, he joined the program.

Brady and Craig arrived at the beach and stood down as close to the water as they could without soaking their shoes. This was where Craig liked to go every time, as though tiptoeing to the precipice of some sacred and terrible moment.

Brady looked at the sun as it slowly rose over the Atlantic.

"Should get to work soon," Brady said after a while.

"I know," Craig said and spit. "Just want to take it in a little longer."

Neither man said anything for some time. There was a special dimension to the silence, Brady could tell. Stewing fragments twitching their way slowly into solemn thoughts. Brady turned to his friend.

"You lied to me before." He could see Craig swallow. "About the boxes. Didn't you?"

"Yes," Craig said right away then looked off in the other direction, his eyes seeming to bob along with the tide. Brady waited for him to say more.

"I shouldn't have walked away that night," Craig said eventually, quietly, cryptically. "The water covered me head to foot."

Brady shook his head in disbelief. "You told me—"

"Yeah, but now I'm telling you the truth," Craig interrupted, looking directly at him. "And the truth is that when I passed out here next to the water the tide did come in and it did wash over me and I was well under the surface, probably for a long time. Probably for half the night."

Brady's eyes connected with the sun hovering just above the Sandy Hook peninsula. "That's just what you *think* might have happened."

"I was under, Brady," Craig insisted. "I was completely unconscious, dead to the world, and then I was underwater."

"So, you're saying?"

"I died," Craig asserted. "Yes. I was underwater for a long time and before long I was dead."

"Then who am I talking to right now?"

"A man who got up and walked away the next morning. Newly sober and alive," Craig replied. He didn't say anything more for several moments then continued, "Somewhere out there is a hole in the water that's exactly my shape and size. And it's the hole I fell through that night. And it's the same hole I've lived in ever since." Craig nodded to himself then spit into the sand. He ground the wad with his heel then sighed heavily. "But I need to leave it behind now."

"What?"

"All of it," Craig gestured around him. "The beach. The bay. I need"—He took a breath—"Deb and I are moving. Arizona."

Brady looked at him hard. "Like for good?"

"'Fraid so."

"What are you going to do out there?"

Craig twisted the toe of his sneaker into the sand until he burrowed a firm cavity. Brady noticed an empty horseshoe crab shell lying upside down like an old helmet blown clean off a soldier's head.

"Too much death," Craig muttered.

"Too much death," Brady echoed, auditioning the words.

"I came across this thing once," Craig said, straightening. "Not sure where I heard it exactly. Supposedly something the Samurai believed. If you ever have to choose between life and death, choose death."

"And why the hell would you do that?" Brady asked.

Craig looked at him. "Cause then you'll no longer be afraid."

Brady thought about this for a few moments. "So, then, what about you?"

"What about me?"

"After what happened, are you still afraid?"

Craig coughed and then took a long, deep breath of the ocean air. "I can still be your sponsor," he offered. "In the sense that you can always call me, day or night."

"I appreciate that," Brady said quietly, his head bowed.

"I know it's not ideal this early into your recovery, and I'm gonna set you up with someone good who can fill in for me when I'm not around. All we have is each other. No one else gets it. If they haven't lived it, they don't get it. Cause it's actually not living, is it? It's dying. If you haven't been to the land of the dead. I mean, that changes you. So, I'm not gonna leave you hanging," he said firmly. "I'm still gonna be there for you even if I'm not there, and there's good people in the group who can pick up the slack. Most important thing is to keep at it. Good days and not good. And there's a lot more of the second kind than the first. But you gotta keep working that program. Work it.

Every day. It's there. Keep working it. That's all there is. The working is living. It's everything. Every day and every night. Again and again and again and again. Over and over and over and over. Sound okay?"

Brady looked at him but didn't say anything further. The sun was climbing higher and higher in the sky, and time was escaping.

"I wish it wasn't today. Goddammit!" Craig kicked the sand. "Wasn't supposed to tell you like this on the day your dad..."

"It's okay," Brady said, eyes trained forward.

"No, it's just. Shit. This morning wasn't supposed to be about..." Craig braced his fingers at his temples. Brady could hear a tremor in his voice that presaged tears. "I know how hard it is. You and I always had that in common. Left by our old men around the same—"

"Stop right there," Brady demanded. "My dad didn't leave. He was laughed out of our house. But not before my mom and sister made sure they'd wiped away any scrape of pride or dignity he still carried after losing his job. Always expecting more. Always demanding more. Well, they weren't working either, the two of them. But they blamed him for everything that went south—*everything*. Is it any wonder he drank the way he did? Night after night. Is it any wonder he stopped bothering to get up and do anything? Any wonder he stopped knowing how to even dress himself?"

Brady turned away slightly. It was always the clothes that overwhelmed him. The coat he would lay over his father when he fell asleep on the porch at night or in the hallway during the day. Or the boots his father had left behind the night he left for good—the bad night, the worst in a long time, shortly after Brady's eighth birthday. The night when he and Brady's sister had started screaming at each other uncontrollably after she had left the back door open too long, letting the moths in. The two of them, toe to toe, their faces purple. The words they spewed at each other were as fast and filthy as the moths.

Then she spat in his face, and their father, in turn, sent his fist through hers. The police came then, but no one went with them. And before long, the house was quiet again, and the moths were nowhere to be found.

Later, when his father had gone out to the tavern, Brady stayed up waiting for him, using the time to try and smoke the moths out of the pantry where he assumed they'd landed. He had turned the lights on and then off again, over and over, trying to lure them into one of their clumsy frenzies so that he could crush them with a paper towel. Only he never managed to find them, and his father never came back inside. Instead, Brady's father had untied his boots and left them roped around the mailbox where Brady found them the next day. Brady had kept the boots safe for his father's return. But years later, after the homeless shelter called to inform him that his father was in the hospital, Brady arrived at the emergency room to find his father's hole-ridden socks uncovered and cursed himself for forgetting the boots at home. The thing that filled Brady with the most pride, and also the most rage, was that his father had had to wear his son's shoes instead of his own at the moment of his departure.

Brady felt Craig's hand creep over his right shoulder.

"Gonna be okay?" Craig asked, his brow furrowed, his voice gentler.

"Yup," Brady said without looking back at him then started hiking up the beach. He climbed the steps that would lead him to the street and back along Craig's sober mile for the last time.

Swim practice would start late as usual. Brady arrived at the pool that afternoon before the bus did. The high school didn't have its own pool, so his team had to commute down to Asbury Park for practice twice a week. Once parked, he saw a message from Karen.

"Don't forget the steaks xoxo."

The goddamn steaks, Brady thought.

He leaned his head back and closed his eyes then reached behind the passenger seat, feeling around for the potted Geranium. He pressed his thumb gently into the soil then moved his fingers to the laces of one of the boots. A moment later, he opened the glove compartment, took out and uncapped the bottle, and drank. The bus appeared in the rearview mirror. He screwed the cap back on and put it away then took a swig from his water bottle and swished the liquid around thoroughly before swallowing.

During the warm-up 400, Brady was pacing alongside the pool when he spotted one of his captains, a senior named Justin, coming out of the locker room with his towel draped around his neck, in no rush whatsoever to begin practice. Justin dropped his bag on one of the bleachers, took out a notebook, and jotted something down.

"Will you be joining us today, Mr. Davis?" Brady called across the pool, his voice competing with the ruckus of splashing arms and legs. Justin held up a finger to indicate that he'd be there shortly.

"Smartass," Brady muttered. In his freshman year, Justin had been the team's MVP. He still had the best butterfly stroke, but he'd long since yielded MVP to the more dedicated swimmers. He'd put on weight, especially in the past year since he had joined the drama group at the high school. The drama kids were rehearsing for the spring musical, *Godspell*. The cast had worn their flamboyant hippie costumes to school one day to promote the play, and Justin had come to Health class wearing rainbow suspenders and a tie-dye shirt. Brady had spotted a couple of boys pointing and mocking Justin behind his back. "He's in the play!" Brady reprimanded, and the boys immediately looked away. Justin, though, had appeared unmoved by his teacher's intervention, and Brady had felt disappointed.

He watched Justin as the boy left the bleachers and approached the starting block. Brady met him as he was about to climb up and placed his fingers on his chest. Drops of water tumbled onto his arm from the glass ceiling.

"What's up, Coach?" Justin asked.

"Gary's not cutting it with the 500," Brady said. "He's come in second to last or last in the past four meets. I want you to take over for him against Manasquan next week. Can you do that?"

"I'm not so good at distance."

"Can you do it?" Brady repeated.

With a shrug, "Sure. I'll try."

Brady narrowed his eyes to Justin's stomach.

"Wouldn't kill you to try to lose a few in the meantime."

Justin looked at the ground and nodded sullenly. Moments passed, but Brady's fingers remained on the boy's chest. Justin lifted his eyes.

"Should I warm up?" he asked.

Brady withdrew his fingers and nodded sideways at the pool. Justin dove in then and sprinted away.

———

Hours later, after the bus dropped the kids off at the high school, Brady pulled into the lot and waited. He checked his watch. Ciccarelli's would only be open for another half hour.

The steaks. Shit.

He watched as the kids left with their parents or friends or in their own rides until Justin was the only one remaining. His parents were always late, and Brady knew that they couldn't afford to give him his own car. Brady took two more swigs then climbed out and approached the bench where Justin was seated.

"Hey, Coach," he said when he saw Brady. "What are you—?"

"Don't worry about what those boys said," Brady interrupted.

Justin looked confused. "What who said?"

"Those punks in class. The ones who were laughing."

"Oh," Justin said, then shrugged and smiled. "They're just not theatre buffs."

Brady put his hands on his hips and looked around the lot then back at Justin.

"Know why I stood up for you?" he asked.

Justin didn't respond for a moment then eventually shook his head.

"I used to act," Brady explained. "I was in every school play. Every single one."

"Really? You?"

"Yes. For years."

"So, what happened?" Justin asked.

"Too many"—Brady searched for the word—"propositions."

Justin appeared confused, and Brady realized that such language carried very little meaning anymore.

"You should keep at it," Brady said finally. "What you do on stage. Keep doing it. No matter what. You'll be the best one day if you keep at it like that."

Justin gave a short laugh and shook his head adamantly. "That's not true."

Brady stepped toward him suddenly, causing Justin to straighten quickly and lean back.

"It's true," Brady said, bending down. "People are going to tell you to stop. Going to tell you to do something else. Be something else. Want something else. Act some other way. Tell 'em to drop dead. They don't know you. They don't know what you have. What you are. Everything that you are and everything that you're not. Don't ever stop. EVER!"

Justin stared at him. After a long beat, Brady took a step back. The wind was shrill, amplified by the dead silence between them.

"The trick to swimming the 500," Brady began, "is to just keep raising those arms. Even when they're so tired and so heavy that it feels like they're not even there. Even then. Just lift them and slide them into the water in front of you. One after the other. Even when it feels like they're coming off, even when they feel numb and like there are thousand-pound weights tied to each wrist. When it hurts to lift. Hurts to bend. Hurts to breathe. Just keep lifting those arms. Keep turning that head. Keep moving in that water."

Justin stared, unable to muster even a slight nod, then his eyes fixated with obvious relief on a pair of approaching headlights.

"Goodnight," Brady said then turned and walked back to his truck. He looked again at his watch.

Those fucking steaks. Those goddamn fucking steaks.

"Don't come back for me," Brady had said to the emaciated man with the dirty face and the dirtier clothes—the man who had been his father—as he lay writhing on the hospital bed, too weak to open his eyes all the way. "Don't wait, just go. It's okay. Go ahead. Just go." Then Brady recalled the last night he and his father had lived in the same house, the night of the moths, the ones Brady had never found and would curse until the day he died. It occurred to him there, strangely, sitting by his father's bedside, that the moths, in fact, might have been inside this man all along. And he waited, absurdly but also somewhat expectantly, for the moths to slip out with his father's faint, final breaths so that he could crush them once and for all. "Don't wait, just go. It's okay. Just go ahead."

Twenty-two years later to the day, Brady slurred his truck into the parking space outside Ciccarelli's. He could see the store was closed, but he came to get the steaks, and he wouldn't leave without them. The inside was dark except for the glow of the beverage case. He could see movement behind the counter. Men were putting plastic wrap over long trays of meat. Brady tried the door. Locked. One of the men looked up at him and shook his head. Brady banged on the frame. The man shook his head more emphatically then came around the counter and stood before the door with his hands on his hips. Brady recognized him as the owner: a tall, heavy man with a thick mustache that prompted some of his customers to call him "the Walrus."

"We're closed," the Walrus said loudly. "You'll have to come back tomorrow."

"Order for O'Sullivan," Brady countered.

The man scratched his forehead, adjusted his glasses, and sighed. He unlocked the door, at which point Brady tried pushing in, but the Walrus stopped him.

"Sir. I've closed the register for the night. I can't make any transactions right now."

"There are five or six steaks waiting for O'Sullivan. My wife phoned them in."

"They'll be here tomorrow. They're in the fridge, don't worry. They'll be just—"

"Will you get my goddamn meat, man!" Brady barked.

The Walrus lifted his chin. Brady felt confident that he could take him if he had to.

"Sir," the owner began.

"Oh, Christ." Brady removed his wallet and took out a hundred. "Here, take it."

"Mr. O'Sullivan, as I have explained—"

"Look I don't care about the change. Keep it. I don't care."

"Were you planning on grilling them tonight?" the owner asked. "Is that the issue?"

"The issue is that I want the steaks my wife ordered, and I don't care how much I overpay for them."

"Well, I'm not about to take that much money off you. I'm pre-pared to make the transaction on the clear condition that this is a one-time-only thing."

"Okay." Brady quickly agreed.

"We have opening times just like everyone else that need to be—"

"Okay!" Brady stuck the money through the door. The owner took it, keeping his eyes on Brady the whole time. From his own wallet, he pulled out some smaller bills and handed them to Brady.

"It's not exact change, but I'm prepared to go down a bit on the price to make this go mor—"

"Should I say thank you?" Brady spat. "You want me to say thank you for doing what I'm paying you to do?"

The owner sighed then closed and locked the door again. Moments later, he returned with the package. He handed it to Brady, who grabbed it and ran to his truck, tossing the steaks on the backseat and looking up to see the towering figure still standing at the doorway. His hands on his hips. Brady, keeping his eyes steadily on the Walrus, reached into the glove compartment and removed the bottle. He took a drink then started the engine defiantly and drove away. Minutes later, his phone rang. Karen.

"Hey, everything okay?" she asked, a slight quiver in her voice.

"Terrific," he replied.

"Get held up?"

"I got the steaks if that's what you're worried about. They're sitting right here next to me."

"I hope it wasn't too much trouble."

"Look, I got the goddamn things, so what more do you want?"

She didn't say anything for several seconds.

"Are you coming home now?" she finally asked. "The kids are wondering—"

"Tell them I'm fine," he nearly shouted.

"Brady, what is it?"

"Everything's fine. Just tell everyone to relax. I'm on my way."

"Okay, but—"

He threw the phone down on the seat and soon after passed a sign for the Parkway. He thought about what Craig had said to him earlier that day. About the land of the dead.

Before long he turned onto the southbound ramp and drove and drove and drove. His phone rang and rang, but he didn't answer it again. He could hear the texts pile up. Eventually, he glanced at the screen.

Karen: "On your way?" "Getting worried" "Did something happen?" "Brady plz call me I'm really worried." "Okay, I'm calling the police."

Brady cracked the side window and hurled the phone onto the side of the highway. He turned on the radio then turned it off again right away. He closed his eyes and pressed his foot harder on the accelerator. He drove at high speed with his eyes firmly shut. He opened them again eventually, but the nearest car was still a ways ahead of him, and he started to decelerate. Still, he drove and drove. He saw the signs for Atlantic City. He took the exit when it came up without knowing or caring why.

Shortly after entering the city, he parked in front of a store with a sign out front that read "We Buy Gold." Brady glanced at his wedding ring but then decided he had enough money in his account for the time being. Brady stepped into a liquor store to use the ATM. He took out a few hundred. Then he took out a few hundred more. When he tried to take out even more, a notice appeared on the screen saying he had "insufficient funds." Brady cursed and slammed his palm against the screen, causing the machine to lift up and then rock back with a loud thump. The guy working the register yelled at him in a heavy accent to "quit it." Brady cursed at him, and the two exchanged a string of unpleasantries until Brady exited the store. Brady then reentered to purchase a bottle, which the same guy grudgingly bagged and sold to him. Within minutes Brady emptied half the bottle and stashed the rest in his truck.

Shortly after, he entered a bar and climbed onto the nearest stool. The bartender was a stocky Black man with a shaved head who was talking to another guy a few stools down. He was considerably shorter than the guy at Ciccarelli's, though Brady felt less confident that he could take him. Brady waved at him. The bartender lifted his index, the way Justin had during practice.

"Smartass," Brady muttered again but too loudly this time.

The bartender looked at him briefly then leaned closer to the guy he was talking to, then eventually he straightened up and came over to Brady.

"How you doin' tonight? What can I get you?"

"What's your name?" Brady asked.

"I'm Russel," the bartender answered. "Is everything okay?"

"Hunky fuckin' dory." He paused. "I'll have a beer."

"What suits you?" Russel asked.

"You choose."

"Draft or bottle?"

"Draft. If you can pour it right." Russel furrowed his brow then seemed to decide that Brady was joking, relaxed his face, and smiled. He brought Brady the beer and told him to enjoy. Brady finished it quickly then asked for another.

"Might want to slow down, partner," Russel advised.

"Think I'm a lightweight?" Brady challenged.

"I think you'd already had a few when you came in here," Russel said in a low voice.

"And?"

Russel spread his hands along the edge of the bar and leaned forward.

"And if I think you've had too much, I'm gonna say so, or I might tell you to leave. So, a word of advice while you're a guest in my bar. Mind your manners, say 'please' and 'thank you,' and know your limit."

Russel straightened up and started to walk away.

"Wash your hands recently?" Brady asked suddenly.

Russel turned. "I beg your pardon."

"When was the last time you washed your hands?"

Russel didn't reply, only kept his eyes on him. A few of the other men at the bar turned their heads.

Brady continued, "You should wash your hands regularly. With soap. It's hygienic."

Russel stiffened then nodded to himself, clear now about who he was dealing with.

"Sir," he began. "There won't be another beer. You're welcome to finish the one you're drinking, then I'm gonna ask you to get the hell out of my bar."

"And if I don't pay?"

"Then there's gonna be a problem," Russel said calmly.

"Like what?"

"Cops might have to get involved," Russel explained.

"And you think that's gonna go worse for me?" Brady said.

"Aw man, go on and get out of here," one of the other customers yelled. Brady eyed an older man with a red beard wearing a frayed denim jacket.

"Someone talking to you?" Brady called. A couple of other guys dismounted their stools. The room was slowly coalescing into a fist that was pointing directly at him. Brady finished his beer in one gulp, took out a couple of hundred-dollar bills, and dropped them on the counter.

"I'd say that's what we might call over-tipping," Russel said when he saw the money.

"For your trouble." Then Brady left.

He passed a group of teenagers on the sidewalk and bumped into one of their shoulders. The guy stared at him but didn't say anything.

"What's that?" Brady called after them, but they kept moving and didn't turn back. Brady decided he didn't want so much cash in his pocket. He went back to his truck and took off his sneakers to stash the money. It was then that he remembered the boots. Removing them from under the passenger seat, he stuffed the cash at the side and wedged his foot in beside the bills, tied them up again, and leaned his head back. He felt dizzy and thought for a moment that he might get sick but then the feeling passed. He looked down at the potted Geranium on the floor, picked it up, and ran his thumb along the petals, plucking out the brown ones the way Craig had explained.

Why did I say that to that guy? Brady then asked himself. *Why did I tell him to wash his hands? I didn't need to say that. I don't give a shit. So why did I say that?*

A couple of guys who looked to be about his age walked by just then. One wore sunglasses and a yellow Yankees cap, and the other wore camouflage shorts and a black sweatshirt rolled up to reveal two full sleeves of tattoos. The guy in the shorts noticed the flower Brady was holding and said, "That for me?" as he passed. Brady stood and followed them for a few paces then pivoted and hurled the plastic pot at the back of the guy's head as hard as he could. There was an explosion of soil, and the guy lurched forward, cradling his head and yelling at the top of his lungs. Then he threw his sunglasses to the street, turned, and rushed Brady, pinning him to the hood of Brady's truck. He pummeled the side of Brady's head. At one point, Brady managed to lean up and shout, "That all? C'mon! That all?" The guy then slammed Brady's face with everything he had. When Brady's vision returned, he was alone on the pavement with his nose in a disc of dried chewing gum. A small pool of blood just above his chin appeared to ripple with his breath.

Brady tried to say something, but his throat wouldn't allow any sound to escape except a thin wheeze. He got to his knees and followed the trail of loose soil along the pavement until he found the nearly empty pot and the dislodged flower with its thin, delicate roots poking out. He pulled the loose dirt off the ends of the roots, trying not to snap even a single strand in the process. He saw the petals tumbling across the sidewalk and began collecting as many as he could, taking up the red and leaving the brown to scatter away in the breeze. With the petals in his hands, he decided that they too should be kept someplace safe. He took off his other boot and deposited the petals over the sole, along with the money, then put his foot back in and laced it up again.

The pain at the side of his face began to sink in. Brady remembered the steaks in the backseat and reached behind him to fetch the package. He unwrapped the raw crimson beef, crumpling the paper into a ball and dropping it to the asphalt then held the meat to the side of his face to ease the swelling. He'd never done this before and had no idea whether it would work. He reached into the glove compartment, took out the bottle, and drained it of its remaining contents. When he heaved the empty up over the roof, Brady listened as it shattered somewhere in the middle of the street.

Eventually, he stood, leaving the door open, and stumbled to the nearest hotel with the beef still pressed against his face. He walked through the sliding doors of the Hard Rock Hotel & Casino. A wave of air conditioning smothered him. He went to the front desk, and a pretty woman with light brown skin looked up right away. She saw the meat and the bruises beneath and pursed her lips.

"Sir? Is everything—?"

"This the casino?"

The woman shuddered, probably from his breath.

"This is the Hard Rock," she replied, making eye contact with a colleague down at the other end of the desk who was staring at Brady with one hand on the counter and the other positioned somewhere behind it.

"This was his once, yeah?" Brady slurred.

"I'm sorry, Sir, I don't—"

"This was the Trump Taj Mahal, wasn't it?"

The woman lifted her chin slightly. "This property used to be a Taj Mahal hotel, yes. That has since gone bankrupt and is now the Hard Rock. Would you like me to call you…?"

"Promises were made," he hissed. "Promises." He paused. "I'm fine, thanks." Brady stalked away, lowering the meat from his face, and dropping it in the first gold-colored trash can he passed.

He trailed the sound of ringing slots onto the floor of the casino. The shrill, cranky noises filled his ears—whirring, rattling, clanging—bearing a considerable weight, as though his head were being filled with sand. At the slot machines, Brady beheld row after row of the elderly. Men and women with frizzy white hair inserting coins and pulling levers and reaping tiny rewards, or else losing what little they had to burn. Brady stumbled across the floor and rammed into a young woman carrying a tray of glasses that collapsed to the ground. Broken glass and ice cubes spread across the carpet, and the woman cursed, then groaned, then looked at him for apology and assistance. Brady mumbled something incoherent then continued on past the restaurants and out, finally, to the boardwalk.

The dark plain of the Atlantic stretched before him. A group of young people passed him. There was a girl between them whose arms were draped around the shoulders of one of the boys and one of the other girls. She looked like she would faint or vomit any second.

"Hey!" Brady called to them, but they didn't acknowledge him. "Hey!!" he shouted, and then they turned.

"Are you gonna take care of her?"

The boy holding up the girl squinted and shook his head as if not comprehending.

"Are you gonna take care of that girl? You better! You better take care of her! Nothing can happen to her, you hear me? All of you—do you hear me?! ARE YOU GONNA PROTECT HER?!"

The boy gripped his crotch and spat. "Fuckin' bum," he muttered, then the group turned and continued along the boardwalk.

Brady started to follow but soon veered off down a flight of stairs and onto the beach. He stomped down to the water's edge. He reached his hand out toward the horizon, tried to close his fingers around it as though signaling to another world, beckoning to it, attempting to hasten its collision into his own. He tried to howl, but nothing came out except a low snarl. He turned and hiked back up the beach toward the spinning lights of the boardwalk. He got to the stairs, but then his foot missed the first one, and he fell to his knees next to the railing. Then he hoisted himself back to his feet and maneuvered instead down along the beach until he found a space to crawl between the pilings. He mushed across the sand, beneath the patchwork shadows filtering down from the amusements and the sound of the people tromping along the planks above.

He went as far back as he could, as though moving through a cave, then Brady sank down and lay on the cold sand littered with countless cigarette butts, plastic cups, and other debris of nightly abandon. He could see people moving above him, but the sound felt increasingly remote. He rolled his head back and forth in the sand the way his father had in the hospital bed. He closed his eyes then opened them again, and that's when he saw the moths, at last, tumbling along the underbelly of the boardwalk, swarming between the planks, their wings beating so fast they looked like fur. Brady wrestled himself into a sitting position then reached down and yanked the boots off one by one, and threw them into the shadows. He heard a light rustling and knew that the petals, and most likely the bills as well, were blowing away. He knew that the moths and the petals were swirling together in the wind, an exchange of scintillant red interlacing with dusty darkness, interweaving then unstitching, tugging and drifting and seldom touching, over and over, their very tension the night's most stable tendon. Neither element was victor, and neither element could ever be vanquished. They were only there, suspended permanently in the dark, carving a shape for Brady for when the flood waters finally arrived. He dug his bare heels into the sand, and there was nothing left: no sight and no sound. He plummeted to the bottom of some forgotten chasm, settling with a soundless thud onto a bottom whose contours were unknown and unnamed.

I was supposed to be someone, and I never found him, he thought. *I was supposed to do something, but I never did it. But I no longer know who that was supposed to be or what he was supposed to do. And that's okay,* Brady realized, shuddering with relief. *That's all right.*

And in that moment, Brady was no longer afraid.

BLIND SPOTS

Terry sees everything. The bus pulling up to the stop on the highway, opening its doors then closing them again, taking on no one. It will continue on down the highway through North Middletown, then through Keansburg, passing liquor stores and children's parks and gas stations, passing windowless strip clubs and boat yards and sad, tired bars. He sees the grass median of Route 36, dotted with yellow flowers that are pawed at and bullied by the shrill wind coming off the bay. A tattered blanket lying on the grass reminds Terry of the one he used to carry around as a child. His mother recently sold it during a yard sale. Terry had briefly protested but caved at his mother's insistence that there was no reason to hold on to the past. Terry was a teenager after all, having recently turned 16, and the past, according to Terry's mother, was simply too painful to keep in their house. Staring at the highway median, Terry can't help but wonder now whether the blanket he sees is his after all.

Terry sees the cars hurling past. He sees the blinking purplish screen of the ATM in front of the nail salon, which used to be the video rental store back when such things existed. He sees the steady stream of patrons passing through the jingling glass doors of the liquor store between the pizza place and the Dollar Tree. He sees the potbellied white man with yellow stains under his arms hawking a snot rocket from the balcony above the China Palace, where, inside, workers scrub oil from cooling stoves and communicate in a language Terry cannot understand, but it awes him to think that other people actually do.

He sees the WaWa a ways down where, in a matter of hours, men with skin almost as dark as his own will line up and peer this way and that way along the highway, eyes straining beneath faded baseball caps for pickup trucks that are hiring for the day. He sees the Dairy Queen that his father used to manage during the week, before his heart attack, where Terry got to enjoy a cup of soft-serve vanilla with strawberry sauce and colored sprinkles if he could explain to his father at least three things he'd learned at school that day. The Dairy Queen is closed now, on its way to becoming something else, or maybe to remain boarded up and empty like so many other places. Most things change around here sooner or later, except the things that don't. But the bike store holds on, year after year. It is one of the few constants in Terry's life, and that constancy is the very wall upon which Terry is prepared now to break everything that his life has been in order to make it everything that it is not.

"Jimmy come yet?" Gerard asks, pulling Terry from his thoughts. Terry shakes his head. Jimmy Guido, Terry's closest friend and soon-to-be accomplice, is nowhere to be seen, while Gerard, who had not been invited, arrived right on time.

"He coming?"

"Guess so."

A car drives by. The driver appears to turn his head toward them as it passes. Terry stiffens and steps back further into the shadows of the alleyway beside the convenience store where they'd agreed to meet.

"I'm gonna smoke," Gerard declares.

Minutes pass. The car that had passed does not return. Terry tries to relax. He looks at Gerard. "Who told you?" he asks.

"Don't matter," Gerard replies.

"You should mind your own business."

"Who says I'm not."

"This got nothing to do with you."

"Come back with me, Terry," Gerard says earnestly. "Come back, man." Terry doesn't lift his eyes from the back door of the bike shop down the alley. Gerard stands still beside him, his cigarette burning a low orange berry into the night.

"You should put that out," Terry warns. "Someone will see you."

Gerard takes a long drag, then crushes it beneath his sneaker.

On the wall next to where Gerard leans, a daddy longlegs makes its way up along the bricks. Gerard arches his palm back to flatten it. Terry is faster, snatching it by one of its legs and tossing it into the bush just as Gerard's hand comes smacking down onto the hard surface, victimless.

"What did you do that for?" Gerard snaps, shaking his hand.

Terry shrugs but says nothing. Another car passes. He doesn't step back this time.

"What you got against him?" Gerard asks, referring to Red, the owner of the bike shop as well as the Triplex Cinema and a few other places in the area.

He'd own the whole town if he could, Terry fumes. *He'd own the air we breathed and the bones we moved with if he could get it all for a decent price.*

The heart and soul of his domain, though, is the bike shop, his first successful business. His nest. His fortress, to which Terry has long been unwelcome and unwanted.

It had started with the potted plants outside the movie theatre several years ago and a few months before his father's death. While his mother was doing their laundry one afternoon, Terry had studied the poster of a "Coming Soon" feature that he thought would be cool to see with his dad. He mindlessly plucked some pointy needles from the plant, and then, out of nowhere, two large hands grabbed him at the back of his neck and whipped him around to confront a face of meanness the likes of which Terry hadn't seen or known could exist until that moment. A hideous scowl sandwiched between a white beard and thick, sooty eyebrows. A look meant for a man rather than a child.

"Keep your filthy fucking paws off the trees, hear?" Red had hollered. "You touch it again and you're in trouble," he continued, then bent down to Terry's level and whispered in a way that was so much worse than the yelling had been. "Big. Trouble. Punk. Fucking little punk. Understand?" Terry shook and nodded idiotically, then ran across the street, without looking both ways, to find his mother.

He avoided the movie theatre for a long time after that. But in the weeks after his father had passed, he had needed all the noisy distraction he could find. There was only one film playing then that interested Terry. It was an R-rated action flick that his father had said he wanted to see but never got to.

Terry did what his friends usually did to get into R-rated films. He bought a ticket for a lame Disney movie then continued past it to the one he had actually come to see. But on his way to Screen 1, the old man intercepted him, demanding to see his ticket. Terry had opened his mouth, and Red lifted his chin, narrowing his eyes at him. Terry thought about trying to explain. He thought about telling this man what seeing this movie would mean. The words were ready. He looked up and opened his mouth, but the look on the old man's face stopped him. It wasn't anger like it had been with the trees, but something worse. He was smiling. He was smiling because he knew that Terry wanted to explain himself. He was smiling the way that a cat would smile, if it were able, after finding a mouse in the bathtub. He was smiling because he could. Because he wanted Terry to try. He wanted Terry to gulp and stutter. He wanted to have something to laugh about after Terry had gone home. So instead of giving him more than he already had, Terry closed his mouth and pointed his eyes at the dirty red carpet and imagined digging a hole in it and burying his whole self until not a fragment of his body remained above the earth. Red had seized him then by the arm just as roughly as he had grabbed him by the neck and escorted him personally out into the cold rain without refunding his money, as other managers had been known to do in such situations of routine mischief.

Terry had gone home that day and stood in his room with his face pressed into his blue cowboy pillow, cursing and spitting until the pillowcase was hot and damp, wishing for Red the worst of everything. "I hope animals eat his skin!" he'd shouted in conclusion. He froze then, nearly unable to comprehend the depth of his own anger. It seemed so much bigger than anything else in Terry's life. It seemed bigger even than his grief.

Tonight, though, isn't about anger, Terry thinks to himself in the alleyway. Tonight is about getting it: the vintage ten-speed bike in the display window of the shop, shiny and black. The kind they used to make. Just like the one his father had when he was Terry's age, captured in an old photograph that Terry studied every time he visited his grandmother. His father tall and lean, a patch of fuzz where a mustache would eventually grow, his elbows propped over the handles, his eyes looking straight through the frame at a son who doesn't feel now like half the man his father appeared to be back then.

I have to have this, Terry knew. *If I can have this bike, I won't need anything else. If this can be mine, the world can keep the rest.*

He had gone inside Red's shop to ask about it, to negotiate, to sweet talk, to hustle, to... He didn't make it an inch past the threshold. Red was behind the counter waiting for him, as he had been at the movie theatre. His arms folded; his head tilted back. Once again, Terry tried to speak, wanted to explain. But didn't. What was the point? So Terry turned and left.

"And stay out," Red had said behind him, unprompted and un-provoked, at which Terry froze in his steps and balled his fists. He could hear Red uncrossing his arms. But Terry didn't turn around again. He unclenched his fists and let the door jingle shut behind him. Making Red uncross his arms had been enough. But enough wasn't nearly enough. Not then. Now it was time. This night. Now.

The wind smells vaguely metallic, like it might snow any second. Terry draws his arms tighter across his chest, determined not to make any sound whatsoever, not like Gerard whose teeth chatter like a wind-up toy. Gerard coughs, damn him—maybe he wants Terry to get caught after all!

"Once you start down this," Gerard says after clearing his throat, "it only gets hotter."

"What makes you so wise?" Terry asks. "Tryin' to tell me what to do and what not to do."

"What I'm tryin' to say," Gerard attempts, "is that there are a hell of a lot of ways you can go. This right now is definitely one of them, but it was never the one anybody ever pegged for you. 'Specially not your pops."

Terry's jaw tightens.

"Anyone can tell you that," Gerard continues. "So that's what I'm here to say. Jimmy gets here and everything goes off, he just likes running wild, so I figured I had to beat him to it. 'Cause he's gonna tell you one thing but everyone else gonna tell you another, and I'm with everyone else this time. You're a good kid. He's not, but you are, Terry. You are."

"Shut up, Gerard! Get out of here!" Terry nearly yells.

"You coming with me?"

"No."

"I said, 'You coming with me!'"

"I said, 'No!' And if the cops show up, I'm gonna know who called, then—"

"Then what?" Gerard gets in his face. "What you gonna do, Terry?"

Terry lifts his leg and stomps on Gerard's foot. Gerard blows out his cheeks and turns his back. "Shit." He wheezes then curses harder but soon steadies himself.

Terry catches his breath, looks up to see Jimmy running across the street.

Gerard straightens up, limps a few feet then leans back against the wall.

"What up, we on?" Jimmy asks, clasping Terry's hand.

Terry looks at Gerard, then back at Jimmy. "We on," Terry confirms.

They both look at Gerard who shakes his head once, mutters something to himself, then shuffles along the alleyway and soon disappears behind a row of hedges. The two boys look at each other. They look around. They walk across the parking lot. The back door of the bike shop is a closed eye, a sealed casket in the night, and Terry is determined to pry it open, come hell or whatever else might be waiting on the other side. Just then it begins to snow.

The phone next to the bed rings. He switches on the light. Red already knows who it is.

"Annie," he says, picking up, leaning his right elbow onto the pillow while he rubs his eyes. "Is everything okay, Peach?"

Red hears his granddaughter sniffling on the other end.

"Peach. What's the matter?"

"Did I wake you?" she asks eventually.

"No," he lies. He adjusts into a sitting position. "Baby, what's the matter?"

"I didn't want to wake you up, Baba."

"Don't worry about it," he assures her. "Is your mother there?"

"No," Annie says.

Good, Red thinks. She'd just make everything worse. Probably hammered somewhere. Shacked up with some other loser in some dive, some armpit shithole somewhere, fully prepared to have his baby and then let taxpayers pay for the food stamps to feed it.

"Need me to come over, Peach?" She doesn't answer. "Where are you anyway?"

"West Long Branch. I think."

"You think?" Red presses. "Stay where you are. Wherever you are. I'm coming to get you." He stands up, keeping the phone pressed between his ear and shoulder.

"You shouldn't."

"I'm on my way."

"You won't find me."

"Watch me," he insists.

"I don't want you to come," Annie says.

Red pauses before sitting down again at the edge of the bed. "Why not, Peach?"

She sniffles and sobs for a minute. Red waits patiently for her to say more.

"You make things worse," she says at last.

Red is dispirited though not surprised to hear this. It's her mother's poison in her ear, he thinks. All the bullshit she's heard about how he ruined their lives. How he's responsible for his ex-wife's stroke. How everything that ever went wrong in any of their lives is somehow because of his grouchiness and belligerence and selfishness and blah blah blah wah wah wah! And she's gotten it now at long last firmly into Annie's ear, Red stews—Annie, the one person remaining who he is inclined and eager to call family and who in most cases is inclined and eager to do the same, even inviting him over to play those stupid video games that she loves.

Red never got any further along than Super Mario Brothers, which is where the nickname Peach came from, after the princess that Annie always selects as her avatar. Red always chose the little green dinosaur, whatever its name was. When Annie started getting into the more violent stuff, he abstained. Too many memories from the war. Too much frivolity blowing people to smithereens on screen. Young people, he believes, do not benefit from thinking of human life as something you can reset once you reach the next level, something you can do over and over again until you get it right. Do young people understand that there are consequences to pulling a trigger at another human being? Or are they all blinded to human life by now? Are children even children anymore? Or have we erased that? Burned it away like everything else. But Red keeps such thoughts to himself as best he can, because time spent with Annie is really the only time worth spending at all these days.

"I won't make anything worse," he says after a long pause. "I promise."

"She'll get mad at you," Annie replies.

"She won't know I'm involved," Red tries again.

"She always does."

"Peach!" Red's patience begins to slip. "Could you just tell me what's—?"

"He fuckin' hit me okay!" Annie yells. "Are you happy now? He fuckin' hit me again!"

"Who?!" Red demands, tightening his grip on the phone and twisting his knuckles against his thigh, though of course he knows the answer. "The fuckin' loser—"

"Don't call him that!"

"Annie, Jesus, you can't be so—"

"So what?" she baits. "Go on, say it."

Red takes a deep breath. "I just wish you had the sense to stay away from people like that. I thought you were done with this creep."

"He got a tattoo of me. Did it himself. Nothing at all like me. But he did that for me. And I..."

"Peach," Red says gently, running his hand up his forehead and through his white, thinning hair. "You have to understand, people like that—"

"Like what?" Annie says defensively.

"People who have no sense. No direction. Who hurt people. Who hurt angels. Angels like you. They, they don't deserve anything, much less your love. Don't you...?"

"Don't I what?"

"Don't you get how special you are?" He puts his hand up against the side of his face. "Don't you? When you look in the mirror don't you see that the world doesn't mean a goddamn thing unless you're smiling in it, don't you?" Red, despite himself, begins to cry.

"Baba," Annie says, starting to sound concerned.

"I'm okay. I'm okay," Red insists. "I just..." His resolve hardens once more. "I'm gonna find the sonofabitch. I'm gonna find him, gonna stalk him like I would a deer, and I'll gut him like one too."

"Baba, don't," Annie protests.

"I will. Or I'll crush his neck instead."

"You couldn't," Annie says.

"Wanna bet?" Red challenges.

"You're too old," Annie retorts.

Red opens his mouth, then closes it again. *You're too old*, he thinks. You're the man in line at the grocery store that the cashier overlooks. You're in line at the deli only to discover that the last of the macaroni salad is gone because the pretty young thing behind the counter gave an extra generous portion to the stud ahead of you. You're in the parking lot walking behind cars with drivers staring at you in their rearview mirrors wishing you'd get out of the way, if they even see you at all. You're a burden. You're a boarded-up, broken-down house that isn't worth repairing because it'll get torn down before long anyway. You're a shuffling, raggedy old man pushing an empty shopping cart, and everyone knows it. Your ex-wife knew it. Your daughter knows it, and now Annie knows it too.

"I didn't mean it," Annie says quietly.

"Yes, you did," Red replies. "And you're right." He thinks for a moment. "But I think I'd be okay dying for this. I think I have it in me to take down one more scumbag," he says.

"Baba..." Annie begins.

"What is it, Peach?" Red says in as tender a voice as he can muster.

"I love you," she says at last, then immediately follows with, "Please stay away."

She hangs up.

"Peach!" Red shouts. He tries calling her back. She doesn't pick up. He tries again. Still nothing. He has no idea where she is and knows it's useless trying to find out. *Why did she call?* he wonders. *Because she needs you*, he reflects. Because she needs you, but she knows you can't help her, so she's stuck, and so are you, and so is everyone. We're all stuck. Each and every one of us. Stuck in this stinking dead end of this stinking dead world. Stuck and useless.

Red looks out the window. It's begun to snow. He wonders what time it is. *Will she call back? Should I sleep? Should I drive? Should I—*

The clanging from downstairs breaks into his thoughts, and he is on his feet before he can think better of it and heading for the stairs leading down to the store from his apartment.

———

Terry's eyes roam this way and that. "How much longer?" he asks.

Jimmy doesn't answer. His fingers twitch expertly, trying to pick the lock the way he knows how, the way he had gotten into Mike's Deli once after it was closed. White headlights spill along the street on the other side of the building. Terry hugs closely to the wall. He looks to the tiny black window of the apartment like a beady spider's eye up above. He thinks he sees a light flicker from within, but he convinces himself it is a reflection off the highway, or a trick of his mind.

"Got it!" Jimmy announces.

"Shut your loud ass up!" Terry hisses.

"Sorry, Terry. We're in, though."

The door creaks open to reveal rows of tools declining in size from left to right, hanging from little hooks on the wall. Grime and sawdust and oil greet them, a tantrum of smell. The wet snow fizzles at the backs of their necks as they prepare to enter. Jimmy hesitates.

"Let's go." Terry shoves him lightly and follows his friend across the threshold into the store. The boys push the door closed behind them. There's enough light coming in through the display window at the other end for them to navigate as they proceed to the main room. Then, straight ahead, there it is. The ten-speed bike, standing above the rows of lesser objects, upholding the room like a monument, like a priest. Terry moves toward it slowly, transfixed, devoted. He steps up onto the platform occupied solely, in his eyes, by this object, this towering figment, this colossus. He fixes his hands over the rubber-fitted handles and closes his eyes to feel the possession, to have the having.

A car passes outside. Its lights flood the glass. The snow magnifies everything. The world is a hard white blanket beyond the display window. Terry is a hidden ember therein, one who now possesses an indescribable might he has never before experienced. It swells up through him like a tidal current. He is more than anything he ever was or thought he could be. He is bigger than any poster or frame. His story is now more than the sum of blank spaces. He is no longer the character screaming off-screen while the cars crash and the buildings explode. This time he is the hero in charge of shadows. If they choose not to see him, fine. He is a commander of sight because he will decide when and where to be seen. No one will make that decision for him. Not anymore. They will never find it, the ten-speed. And any time Terry passes the bike shop on his way to see a movie, his eyes will briefly engage Red's on the other side of the glass, and he will hazard a smile. For he will know, as Red will know, what only the two of them will ever be able to truly understand: Terry has won.

"HEY!" Jimmy calls from behind the counter. Terry turns to see what he's up to.

"I found the register," he says. Terry wants to say something but can't. Jimmy lifts it up. "I'm gonna get it open," he explains. "You get the bike and meet me out back. I'm gonna find a tool." And with that, Jimmy ducks into the other room.

Terry's hands won't release the handles. His fingers are clenched so tight he can feel them tingling. Another car passes. This time the wash of light nearly blinds him. He arches back, then bends over as though to retch. When the car is gone, he rights himself again. His thumbs are poised at the gearshift, his toes brushing at the pedal closest to him. *This thing, this terrible thing, won't release me*, he understands. The bike's reflection in the glass appears to darken and expand. He sees a hint of his own reflection and thinks of his father.

No, Terry decides. *You will not take me over. I am more than you. I am more than what you are trying to make me. I will let you go. I will let you go once and for all because I'm sick and tired of being small. Smaller than the fear. Smaller than the rage. And now that I've gotten inside I can get back out again. Yes. Outside the fear. Outside the rage.* And with that, Terry releases the handles.

"Terry. Hey Terry," Jimmy calls from the back room. "I almost got it. I just about—" In his excitement, the screwdriver leaps up from his sweaty palm and twists briefly in the air before its inevitable clatter onto the orange tiles which exceed the carpet surrounding the main counter. It bounces four times then rolls in a semi-circle to the bottom of the stairs as if drawn by a magnet. Jimmy whimpers. Terry's chest does a somersault. He listens. Nothing. Blessed nothing. Then. The first. Creak. The second. The third. The fourth. The eighth. The tenth.

"TERRY!!" Jimmy calls then slips back into the darkness of the workroom and out the back door. Terry finds his feet and starts across the floor, stumbling down from the display area. He sees the back door open to a world of snow. A door opens somewhere above. He trips.

There is a crash. Terry sends a row of bikes toppling over. He gets to his feet. He—

"Stop right there!" Red commands at the bottom of the stairs.

The old man enters the room, his arm outstretched, the object it clutches yearning with purpose. The cylindrical barrel catches the frosted light spilling in through the back door. Red steps over the screwdriver toward Terry. The object he holds bores a hole in the room through which Terry is sucked out as though at high altitude.

"Don't move a muscle," Red commands. He steps closer. The scrapes of light at both ends of the room reveal their faces to one another in full. Hateful recognition twitches in Red's countenance. His back straightens with new resolve. "You shouldn't be here," he grits between his teeth.

Terry lifts his chin. He knows that words are useless. Red already believes everything that he wants to. Terry is already the negative space. Everything that Red cannot see, one of his many blind spots. But Terry will not raise his hands, because they are his...

"Damn you," Red growls, raising the object higher.

...and he will not give Red his mind...

"Damn you, you scumbag sonofabitch asshole punk!"

...because it is free.

"This is mine. You hear me! This. Is. Mine!"

"Yes," Terry confirms. "You hold everything that you hold, and my hands are empty."

The old man raises his hand, the teenager raises his head. Every color and non-color in the room collapses.

Terry sees everything. The balcony. The stores. The bars. The strip clubs. The children's parks. The boatyards. The cars and trucks and the men lining up for work behind them. He sees yellow flowers stem deep in gray snow along the highway's median, and a child's blanket buried somewhere underneath. He sees another bus open, then close its doors again. Still taking on no one.

LONG GRASS

I t's all for show, Kathleen knows as she pulls up at the train station where Ann is thumping her foot on the platform with her arms crossed. She can't have been waiting *that* long.

Opening the door, "Ann I'm so—"

Ann, right away, "Where were you? Did you forget what time it was scheduled to arrive? Are you stupid? Are you brain-damaged?!"

The questions come as they usually do, like bullets. Kathleen doesn't say a word, just drives.

"How is he?" Ann asks after she's had a chance to calm down.

"Okay, thanks," Kathleen replies. "Recovering, I guess."

"Sick?"

"Bad back."

"What else is new?"

"Also, probably, I guess, the reviews—"

Ann laughs. "You mean he actually gives a shit about that, ahem, theatre critic?"

"It's *Two River Tribune*. They have a lot of influence over what goes on to Red Bank Rep."

"I know. I know. Y'all's regional fun house." The Arkansas in Ann always comes out most aggressively before seeing Kathleen's father, as though she needs to shake it out before folding it away.

Ann rolls down the window and pulls out her Marlboro Golds. "Mind if...?"

"Go ahead."

They will soon turn onto the dirt road which will lead them to Kathleen's childhood home and Ann's Big Daddy.

"How was the audition?"

"Called back for something with Provincetown."

"That's good."

"It's okay. And I've done some readings with a hot young downtown company that got some stellar reviews recently. So, they're doing *Streetcar* this season. The *Streetcar* you've never ever seen before. BD would like it, lots of drugs, lots of fighting, and lots—oh lordy—*lots* of fucking!"

"Uh-huh."

"But it's gutsy. It's bold. It's a new take."

"Would you play Blanche?" Kathleen asks.

"Of course, I'd play Blanche!" Ann snaps, as though the question is outrageous.

"You've got a lot of irons in the fire."

"Thanks, Mom."

"Sorry."

"Stop apologizing. And stop using old-ass expressions that make you sound like a hag. You're what, 21?" Kathleen nods. "Well, as your senior of three years, let me tell you, with compassion, responsibly, darling: *stop trying to be* SO GODDAMN OLD *already*!"

They turn off the main road onto the driveway. The car snakes between slopes of high grass that bow with the wind toward the trees, shaggy from last night's rain, which bracket the property, the woods against which the redness of the house stands out like a blister.

"Why won't he pave this already?!" Ann asks.

"That would be inauthentic for him—"

"Yeah, I get it, since he's moved to the backroads, he needs to keep this Thoreau shtick, right? Shit!" Ann yelps, brushing the ashes of the cigarette off her skirt which leave a charcoal comet tail in their wake. "Can you watch it?"

"I can't help the bumps," Kathleen protests.

"You can help driving like a fucking idiot though, right?" Ann shoots back and groans while beating her skirt. It's likely that she's smoothing the stain deeper into the fabric, but Kathleen keeps this to herself. Kathleen slows to a crawl as they near the house and parks next to the side porch where BD emerges momentarily, hands stuffed in his khaki shorts, eyes bent to the floor as they generally are. This gives him an unfortunate stoop, a monkish posture abetted by the expanding dome of baldness. Pools of early August sweat have already begun to hatch beneath his arms.

Ann does not close the door after leaping out. "The house looks terrific!"

"I was thinking the same about you, Baby Blue," he says, a nickname based on her eyes.

They wrap arms around each other and kiss on either cheek as is customary, as is European.

"Train late?" he asks Kathleen.

"No. I was though, a little," Kathleen says after closing both doors.

"Iced Tea and chess!" BD announces right away. "Should that be our strategy today?"

"Oh BD, boring!"

"Baby Blue, you almost won last time. You had me in check twice!"

"You took pity."

He makes a scout's honor sign. "I did no such thing. You're a better strategist than you think. You conceive patterns easily, and you guess your opponent well. There's a calculating tiger in you at all times. That's what makes you a sensation on stage!"

Ann puts her hands to her hips and tilts her head. "You're my biggest fan, BD. Sometimes I think you're the only one."

"Only a matter of time." He reassures her as he knows he must.

"I don't mind playing chess," Kathleen mentions.

"No, I think it's too boring for today after all," BD revises. "Let's sit outside and soak it all in."

———————

Kathleen cooks dinner that night. Wild mushroom ravioli, Broccoli Rabe with caramelized onions, and grilled shrimp skewered with sun-dried tomatoes and pine nuts. BD brings out a blueberry pie from a local farmer's market and opens a second bottle of Chardonnay. Ann objects to nearly everything Kathleen has cooked, on the basis of having to maintain her figure ahead of crucial auditions. Nevertheless, she has polished off the first bottle all but single-handedly and is taking the lead with the second as well. Ann takes her glass to the porch swing where BD joins her shortly. The whispers and giggles they share seem to Kathleen to fall into cadence with the locusts and crickets that herald the close of day. The earth and everything it has spawned is chattering and flirting. Kathleen pushes her glass away. Her eyes wander out over the long grass and settle into the last eyelash of the sun hovering over the trees. The river is in the air, and she closes her eyes to allow it to cradle her.

"Everything's dead," she hears her father complain. "Theatre's dead. Poetry's dead. Short stories are dead. The novel's dead. Film is dead. Rock music is dead. Jazz is dead. Blues. Hip-Hop. By now probably even the Internet is dead. Dead! Dead! Dead! Says who, I say! The only people proclaiming that things are dead are overrated hacks. They're the ones who are dead. Not us!"

"How's the novel coming along?" Ann asks.

BD replies heavily, "Dead."

Ann locks her arm with his, rests her head against his shoulder. Moments later she kisses his neck. Moves up to his cheek and then his ear.

"Take me inside," Kathleen hears her instruct.

BD stands up. He tries to conceal the difficulty he has getting up from the swing. He whispers something to Ann as they cross the porch which makes her cackle, holds the door for her, and squeezes her as she crosses into the house. He closes the screen door behind them, and Kathleen is alone on the porch with the crickets and locusts thrumming around her and the shadows hardening into night.

Kathleen twists one of her auburn curls around her ring finger and thinks about what she'd like to do the next day with Ann. So, so many things, but BD won't want to share. It's hard to say who needs who more. The retired director or the would-be starlet. Two creatures of permanent appetite and little to offer besides.

The night is full grown, and the rocking and thumping and groaning and then ecstatic shrieking from the upstairs bedroom tumble down and out the screen door while Kathleen tries as hard as she can to train her ears to the harmony around her instead.

Soon the strangers will come, and she needs to concentrate. Any moment now. They'll come.

———————

Ann emerges onto the porch later to find Kathleen wrapped in a blanket, still seated at the table.

"He's asleep," Ann confirms, settling onto the porch swing. She pulls her cigarettes from her sweatshirt pocket and lights one. "Fuck that's good," she says, sinking more snugly into the cushions. She sucks deeply on the cigarette like it was an inhaler, like it was giving her air rather than diminishing it. Her eyes bore deeply into Kathleen, hot and pointed like the hovering ember she stokes.

"BD promised he would take us to the beach club for dinner tomorrow. Then for ice cream!" Her voice peaks to a gooey, ironic falsetto. "You game?"

"I should clean tomorrow."

"Kathy, I won't be here next weekend, and I want to spend time with you."

"Auditions?"

"There's this Broadway panel I have to organize at the university."

"I didn't know you still worked there."

"Little things here and there. The theatre department can't get much done without BD around. They need him and he needs them."

"You don't think...?" Kathleen starts.

"What?"

"You don't think he did the right thing retiring when he did?"

"I think he thinks he did the right thing. Finally, time to write. Or so he says."

"It was weighing him down," Kathleen says.

"It was also keeping him up," Ann counters. "He loved being the king of the mountain. Don't tell me he didn't. Calling the shots. Deciding where the funding went. Which speakers to invite. Which plays to produce. He got to program every season unchallenged. The other professors were too intimidated. He was always on top. Always conquering. And now…"

"And now?"

Ann sits quietly for a few moments, smoking and thinking. "Creativity is more than conquering, isn't it? It might be part of it, but if you don't know how to surrender, how to give up once in a while…" She stubs out her cigarette in an ashtray on the windowsill next to her, grinding it as though to punctuate a point. "The faculty is blind without him. That's all I can tell you. They're asleep at the wheel. Don't even ask me who's 'in charge' now. The fact is, he may as well still be in charge but instead of being there in the action he's out here, doing this."

"Are you starting to…?"

"Am I starting to what?"

"You're not…"

"I'm not what? Kathleen?"

"Just don't tell me…"

"Kathleen. Breathe."

They're both quiet. The crickets and locusts rattle and somewhere in the distance a siren wails.

Just then BD bangs through the door and nearly trips at the threshold but regains himself at the frame just in time. He makes a strange wheezing sound as though choking on a laugh.

"Are you all right!" / "Thought you were asleep!" the women exclaim.

"Pair of queens!" BD croons, seesawing between his toes and heels as though steadying himself during an earthquake. Then he withdraws two polished items from his pocket—one black, one white—and casts them out over the porch where they make a quiet thump somewhere off in the grass. "Those were the pair of queens. Can't play chess without the queens, now, can we? Who'll get them now? Will you!" He extends his finger toward Ann. "Or you!" to Kathleen. "Who will bring me my queens? Which of you fair, fair maidens will bring me my queens?"

"BD," Ann begins, soft yet directive. "You shouldn't be drinking so much on meds."

"Who said I'm taking meds!" BD roars. "Who the hell do you think...?!" He calms himself. "I'm sorry." He pants. "They're only for the pain," he explains. "Just for the pain of this goddamn"—He begins pounding at his lower back—"old geezer back I've been cursed with!"

"Don't do that, Dad!" / "C'mon BD," the women say in unison.

"I wasn't supposed to get this old this fast. Coming out to the country was supposed to heal me. Supposed to give something back. I thought the city was making me old. Ha! It was *me* making me old. Nothing more. Nothing more." BD lets out a long sigh, looks at one then the other, then throws his eyes out into the darkness of the yard beyond the reach of the porchlights. Moments pass. "We're really making something here. The three of us. Something real," he says, almost savoring the word. "Real," he repeats.

"BD," Ann tries again. BD looks at her. "I'd like to talk to Kathleen alone for a while. Just us girls. Have some leftovers."

"Can I have more pie?" he asks sheepishly. Kathleen tries to convince herself that he's joking.

Ann tilts her head and nods, at once pitying and adoring. "Yes, babe. You can have more pie. Then rest your back a little. I'll be up again soon to tuck you in," she finishes with a flick of her eyebrows and a fast wink. BD does a kind of jig where he stands, a stumble of a dance step before he accedes by shutting the door and leaving the two alone once more.

"He'll be snoring by the time I get there," Ann says once he's back inside.

They sit in silence for a few minutes. Ann lights another cigarette. The locusts continue adding thin layers of warm, rickety music as the night piles in around them.

"Do you...?" Ann begins.

"Do I what?" Kathleen asks.

Ann inhales deeply without finishing the question.

"So, you don't mind still being there?" Kathleen asks.

"At the university?"

Kathleen nods. "Thought you were ready to leave it behind for good."

"Thought I was," Ann says, thumbing the side of her mouth, her elbow propped against the back of the chair so that the thin trail of smoke from her cigarette drifts into her brown wavy hair. "It's warm in there, though," she continues. "Everyone strutting around, so sure they'll be the exception. That's the great cruelty of drama programs, isn't it? They make so much money off of that lie. That you—*you*—will stand out. You will break the mold. You will have what it takes. You are not them. You are not us. You are unique. They make you believe that, so hard. Even when they try to tell it to you straight, even when they break you down, that's always still in the background. This idea that you—*you* are someone special. They have to. It's their reason for being. Why else would they get paid and have tenure and all that shit? But still, it's cruel. And all the same, I miss it. I miss it a lot. I miss looking forward rather than back. And when BD was there. The two of us. They hated me."

"Who?"

"Don't be coy. I know what they thought of me. That I earned those lead roles under BD's desk rather than onstage."

"They didn't..." Kathleen tries.

"Of course, they did. But who gives a shit? I earned those roles, every way I could. But what was it all for? What did it all mean? It was just dreaming into dead ends, wasn't it?"

"Ann, come on. You were—"

"What?"

"Magnificent," Kathleen finishes.

"Don't say that." Ann stabs out her cigarette again but not before lighting yet another with the tip of the old.

"Why are you smoking so much?"

"I just am." Ann stands and walks to the edge of the porch, her arms crossed, the cigarette hovering so close to her face Kathleen is afraid it might singe her eyelid.

"Ann..." Kathleen tries but Ann turns suddenly and steps toward her, her knees pushing against the table so that its legs scrape rudely across the porch boards. Kathleen straightens herself, holding her hands together tightly in her lap.

"What do you do when I'm not here?" Ann asks, the timbre of her voice shifting.

"What do you mean?" Kathleen asks innocently.

"I only come on the weekends. You're here all week, aren't you?"

Kathleen doesn't reply.

"That's not how it started out," Ann continues. "Those weren't the terms. But it's true, isn't it? When I leave on Sunday, you'll stay."

"I have to," Kathleen responds.

"Why?"

"He needs me."

"Do you really think that?"

"Besides..." Kathleen starts to say.

"Besides what?" Ann asks.

"I don't like leaving her," Kathleen explains quietly.

"Who?"

Kathleen juts her chin toward the yard.

"Kathleen," Ann says, following her gaze, "there's no one there. You know that, right?"

"She's there," Kathleen corrects. "She's everywhere."

"Kathleen!" Ann says again more loudly.

"In the air, in the water. But above all, in the grass."

Ann drops the cigarette on the porch, pushes the table aside abruptly, and caves to her knees. She yanks Kathleen's hands out of her lap and folds them between her own. She leans up so that the two are so close that Kathleen can smell the cigarette smoke in both her breath and her hair.

"Kathleen... Kathleen... SARAH!" Ann amends. "Sarah, listen to me!" Her voice changes, the slight Southern accent dissolving into a definite British one. "Sarah, look at me, listen to me."

"I'm not—"

"Sarah, stop it! Listen to me. Your name is not Kathleen. Your name is Sarah. I'm Joanna. You are not BD—you are not *Edward's* daughter. Okay? You are an actress, like me. We're both actresses. We studied together; we roomed together. Right? Right?"

Kathleen stares at her blankly.

"You know all this, don't you?" Ann continues, squeezing Kathleen's hands so hard that she can feel her rings pressing against the bones of her fingers. "We both come from overseas. I'm from London; you're from Australia. Right, Sarah? Right?"

"You're tired," Kathleen offers to which Ann slams her head into their hands and begins to tremble. When she looks back up, Kathleen can see the tears streaming down the sides of her face.

"I never would have agreed. I never thought it would go this far." She sobs, trying to control her volume lest she attract the very unwanted presence and attention of BD. "It sounded—well it was fun, wasn't it? He cast us in his play as sisters. Then he wanted to cast us in something else, only he wouldn't tell us what it was. Only that he wanted to do a rehearsal process unlike any he'd ever done before. He wanted us to disappear into these roles so deeply that we'd become them in our bones. Me, the insecure floozy, you the doting daughter. It was fun; it was fun—and he paid us well with grant money that he wanted nothing to do with, and we were broke—*are* broke. It was something to do and it was weird, and it was fun and even fucking him was fun at first, but..."

"But..." Kathleen continues.

"But it's gone too far. It's gone too deep. And you're not well, Kathleen—*SARAH!* You haven't been for a long time, and this experiment this—whatever it is—is making everything worse."

"Ann," Kathleen says patiently, as though speaking to a child. She runs her tongue between her lips and looks up at the dark porch light where the crusts of dead insects spot the inside of the lamp. She looks down again. "This is where I belong. This is where I was born."

"No!" Ann interjects.

"This is where my mother is buried—"

"SARAH YOUR MOTHER'S ALIVE!" Ann shouts, uncaring about her volume now. She shoots to her feet, moves closer, towering over Kathleen who keeps her hands folded in her lap.

"She's alive and she lives outside Melbourne. And this is *not* where you were born, and it is *not* where you live, and Edward is *not* your father. And he's not your boss, and by now he's not even your director! He was never Head of anything. He waited tables for thirty fucking years then worked as an adjunct for a bit and never really made a dent anywhere. But there we were eating out of his palm because he made us feel good. Because he flattered us and made us feel good and because he..."

Ann puts her hands over her eyes and stomps blindly back across the porch then collapses again in the porch swing, leaning her elbows onto her knees and cradling her head, pushing her hair back and appearing to yank at it from behind. She shakes her head and mutters something to herself that Kathleen cannot hear. Kathleen feels the impetus to rise and comfort her, but she stays where she is. She swallows hard, trying to gather the words. She looks back out across the yard to the trees in the distance, enormous and dark, stalwart as ancient sentinels casting their poise against the flood of night.

"The world out of focus," she hears Ann say. "He's so obsessed with capturing life most authentically onstage. As though the actors shouldn't know they're being watched. Should forget that they're acting. But then it's not acting, is it? If you don't embrace the artifice, what are you left with?"

Kathleen doesn't reply.

"We're not his actors anymore," Ann continues. "If we were, he would have shown us by now."

"Shown us what?"

"The script."

"What script?"

"The script he's supposedly been working on this whole time. The one for us—that he's been using us to write. When he was asleep, I went looking for it. He leaves his notes everywhere, I thought it must be there somewhere."

"You shouldn't have done that," Kathleen objects. "He's very private about his work, especially when it isn't finished."

Ann waves her away. "I know all that rubbish, I know. I found it, though. Our script. Our supposed Meisterwerk. I know because I saw our names at the top, our *real* names. And do you know what was on it? I'll tell you. NOTHING! Bloody nothing! Oh well that's not true, is it? No, there was something. A title. Two words. Long. Grass. That's it."

Kathleen doesn't respond.

"Well, aren't you going to say something?" Ann demands. "Aren't you going to express something—some shock, some anger, some disbelief that we've just been wasting our time at the whim of an old hack who seduced us into playing his maids all these weekends, his—no—his *whores*! Least that's what I am. Maybe not you. Then again"—Ann leans forward in the chair, cocks her head—"What does he give you anyway?"

"Give me?" Kathleen asks.

"Yeah. What is it that he gives you that—?"

"What I was before," Kathleen says suddenly, using Sarah's accent, "was nothing. It wasn't real."

"Wasn't real?" Ann says with a laugh and a flash of relief in her eyes.

"No, not like this. We aren't born real, you know. We have to make ourselves that way. That's what acting is. It isn't pretending. It isn't even expressing. It's creating. Or, rather, recreating. There are times when you have to be unreal until you become real. And that's what I am now."

"Real?" Ann asks incredulously.

Kathleen doesn't reply but stands instead and stretches her arms back and takes a deep breath.

"I'm going to turn in now," she says, reclaiming her other voice.

"Don't do this. Sarah."

"I assumed I'd sleep on the couch. But if you weren't planning to go back up to BD…"

"Jesus you stupid bitch, when are you going to get it through your head—*nobody is watching you right now*! *We're not onstage*!"

"Aren't we, though?" Kathleen replies.

Ann recoils slightly. "What does…?"

"Aren't we, though?" Kathleen repeats, steadying her gaze.

The two women stare at each other for several beats. Ann's face gradually morphs from a scrutinizing tightness to reluctant apprehension. "No," she says.

Kathleen doesn't respond but walks through the door, allowing the screen door to whack shut behind her. On her way to the stairs, Kathleen sees that her father only made it as far as the downstairs sofa. She goes over to him. The television is on, casting blue shadows across his face while he sleeps, making him appear phantom-like beneath the low lights in the living room. His white frizzy hair matted against the pillow, his features coarse and humorless. She strokes his head. He snorts and bucks her hand in his sleep. She waits until he settles again then lowers her hand and tries to pet him once more.

"Baby Blue," he murmurs without opening his eyes. "Is that…?"

"It's me," Kathleen whispers.

"Where is she?"

"I'm here, don't worry."

"You won't leave," he says, his eyes still closed.

"I won't leave you," Kathleen responds. She leans closer to his ear. "You have made me real," she confides. "You have made me me. I wasn't before and now I am." Kathleen kisses his forehead. "You're my father. I'm your daughter. Your real daughter. Not the one who left. The one who stayed. I'm your daughter, and I love you." She kisses his forehead again, then his lips, then stands, straightens her skirt, and turns to the coffee table where she sees the pill bottle on its side, its remaining contents spilled out over the mahogany surface.

I hope he hasn't taken too many, she worries, then screws the cap back on and places the bottle upright. She turns off the television and walks through the house, soaking in its silence, admiring each dark and quiet corner. The house has her fullest attention, and she its. She steps back onto the porch in time to see the headlights coming down the driveway. Her friend meets it halfway, flags it to stop, then opens the door and gets in. Kathleen catches Ann's eye as the car backs up and begins to turn. Neither of them waves. The car drives away, and she is gone, and Kathleen is alone. She steps off the porch and into the grass.

She walks until she feels something pointy and hard beneath her foot. She bends down and picks up the chess pieces that her father had tossed into the yard earlier. Kathleen holds them to her chest and looks out toward the trees, all but black in the distance. The crickets and locusts are quieter now. The earth itself seems to hush as the strangers emerge. They come out one by one, lines of viewers scattered in the dark of the woods, some with binoculars and headsets, some half-dressed, some not dressed at all. They remain at a distance and stare at her as she stares at them. No one is entirely sure who should bow and that, perhaps, is the beauty of this, she realizes. If theatre is dead, Kathleen decides, then let it be for the ghosts.

She lies down in the weeds and looks up at the sky. The stars are wet paper blades, she thinks, not unlike the grass around her. She imagines floating up to meet them, or rather, that one part of her rises while the other sinks below the grass and dirt, below the rock and grain, down past the armor, the hardness, to where the earth shifts, and chuckles, and keeps kind thoughts for the delicate and the damaged. We're finally real, she thinks. And before Kathleen can think another thought, she is asleep.

MELISSA

After a series of tests, the doctor offered his opinion on the cause of the bleeding: that it was a threatened miscarriage and that while the heartbeat was still detectable, within a matter of days it would most likely be gone. As soon as she stepped out of the building into the parking lot, Melissa lit a cigarette. She'd smoked during her last pregnancy and Amy had turned out just fine—perfect even, pink and happy and beautiful—so what the fuck did all the know-it-alls know and what the fuck difference would it make this time anyway?

She hated doctors' offices. You always left feeling like shit about something. Too much of this, not enough of that. Who needs any of it? The Parliament withering between her fingers, she texted Danny to let him know the news. She stopped halfway, right after typing "threatened," and deleted the message. Let him squirm, she decided. Let the not knowing hurt before the knowing helps.

Melissa didn't know whether Danny wanted the child or not. He liked the idea but not the truth of it, Melissa had realized, the same way he sometimes talked about building a house for the four of them, but never said a word or appeared to think much about what it would mean to actually live in it. And anyway, he was the reason she'd had to come here in the first place. Bastard. Fucking piece of shit. He'd punched her after all, right where he knew he shouldn't have, not on the arm or even her face like he had before but right dead center in the gut like the mother fucker that he was. So that Melissa had had to miss yet another shift at the diner to spend the afternoon in the goddamn doctor's office hearing about her threatened miscarriage. No, fuck him. Danny would have to sweat this one for a while. He'd promised to get help. He usually did after nights like that. It was always bullshit. Last night might have been different, though. Last night he may have actually frightened himself for a change. Melissa could see it in his face after she regained herself. His eyes had hurt to look at. Maybe he'd thought about living in that house after all.

Then again, probably not. Right now, he was probably getting high with those loser friends of his who had less going for them than he did if that was even possible. No jobs, no apartments of their own. Only what their girlfriends or their girlfriends' families would give them. It was a hustle, pulled off by a swarm of deadbeats, completely uncoordinated of course. Coordination would actually require them to talk about something other than their dicks. And Danny wasn't even the alpha among them. Shit, not even the beta. He was little more than a fat head and loud-ass mouth trudging around in the pack like a mule. So what the fellas said went. And if they assured him that the bitch had it coming and that he shouldn't feel sorry and shouldn't offer to pay for her doctor's appointment or compensate her for the tips that she missed out on and that he shouldn't try to do anything for anyone else ever, then you better believe that was exactly what he was going to do. In other words, jack shit. So no, he didn't need to know about their baby. Because he didn't actually care, and if he did then Melissa didn't want him to. She didn't want him to want anything from her at all right now.

She thumbed back to her Contacts and sent a message to her mom instead. "Leaving doctor now. Need time to self. Get Amy at bus stop plz." She waited a couple of minutes for the reply. She thought about another cigarette, had hardly touched the first. Her mom saw the message and began typing. Typing, pause, typing, pause. It would be long and tortured, Melissa knew, likely a request for a medical update followed by a lecture on how Melissa needed to pull her weight with Amy after school. Fuck it, Melissa decided and dropped the phone in her bag. She really did need time to herself now. Time for herself. Time to drink.

———————

Melissa ordered a beer along with a Buffalo chicken sandwich that came with waffle fries and celery sticks. She ate the celery first to get it over with. The orange sauce soaking the deep-fried cutlet was way too hot. She'd asked for mild but Frank in the kitchen had either misread her order or goofed. She wasn't about to give anyone a hard time about it. Especially not today. Call it perspective, or some shit like that. Bayside Bar and Grill had only reopened a couple of weeks earlier after undergoing major renovations in the aftermath of Hurricane Sandy. A lot of places along the Shore had decided to close up for good, so these guys had made out pretty well, she thought, all things considered.

Melissa spread blue cheese dressing over her sandwich to cool it down. She took her sweet time with the beer, electing the kind of light, dainty sips she would normally assail as "pussy drinking" if she saw anyone she knew drinking that way. She cut herself slack, though. Tonight may as well be a "pussy drinking" night. No one could accuse her of being a pussy about anything else, after all, and if they did then they better have their running shoes on because she wasn't about to have it.

"Hey Frank," she called over the bar.

Frank was setting two plates down on the pickup counter, each with a barbecue burger and piled high with either onion rings or sweet potato fries. He hit the bell and looked up.

"Sandwich to your liking?" he asked, flipping a grease-stained rag over his shoulder.

"It's great," she replied.

"Really? Not too hot?"

She pressed the thumb and index of her left hand together to form an A-Okay sign.

"Why'd you guys paint over the mural?" she asked.

Frank tilted his head, confused.

"The mural outside on the wall. Why'd you paint over it?"

Frank shrugged. "Everything else was getting redone. Out with the old, I guess. I dunno. Wasn't my decision. I'm just the putz at the grill." He winked. "Why? Miss it?"

"No," Melissa said and took another sip of beer. She put the glass down and gave a light belch. "Yeah, I do," she corrected. "It was. Colorful. What'd it say, "'Greetings from...?'"

"'Greetings from Sea Bright,'" Frank said. "Management thought once upon a time it would attract more tourists. Not sure it ever made a damn bit of difference, though. Same knucklehead locals who came here before still came here after and not a soul otherwise. But I guess 'Greetings from Highlands' didn't quite have the same ring to it. But y'know something, I agree. The colors were nice. Really did look like a postcard from the beach. Had the same layout as the cover of that Springsteen album. Guy they hired to paint it did a great job. So, yeah, I agree. We shoulda kept that up instead of painting over it." He took the rag off his shoulder. "Some shit's worth holding on to, I guess, even if Mother Nature tries to fuck everything up. You let me know if you need a refill on fries or anything."

"I will, Frank. Thanks."

As Frank disappeared back into the kitchen, Melissa dipped a fry into her ketchup cup and munched thoughtfully. She was tipping the edge of the glass to her lips again when a voice interrupted her from down the bar.

"Shouldn't do that, y'know."

Melissa turned to find Chris Byer, another Bayside regular, a few years younger than she was, with shaggy dark hair and wide-rimmed glasses that ate up most of his face and made him appear more childish than smart. "Why the hell not?" she replied.

"You're pregnant, aren't you?" he asked, pushing his glasses up his nose.

Had she told people yet? she wondered. Had she already begun to show? Had Frank noticed? Was that why he was so concerned about what she was eating? He normally didn't give a shit whether or not something he'd cooked was to anyone's liking.

"What if I'm just fat?" she challenged.

Chris widened his eyes, followed by an excited grin.

"If that's the case," he said, "then the next one's on me."

———

In the car, a little less than an hour later, Chris tried and failed repeatedly to undo Melissa's bra. He was drunk; she wasn't.

"Am I... is it...?" He panted.

"You're fine," she encouraged, but she could hear the impatience and growing disinterest begin to slip out. She began rubbing him in small circles while he gasped and twitched then unzipped and took hold. She tolerated his wimpy little grunts, trying to decide where and how—and for a moment even whether—to finish him.

"Wait, wait," he said suddenly. She continued anyway until he pulled back and insisted, "Melissa, stop!" He pressed his back against the passenger-side window, brushed the hair off his forehead, and tried to steady his breathing. Melissa readjusted in her seat and stared at him. The roof of her mouth still tingled from the Buffalo sauce.

"I want to help you," he said at last.

"You want to help me?" she echoed.

"Yes," he confirmed, "I wanna help you, and I think I can." He took a deep breath. "I've seen you," he continued. "I've seen you with your daughter. Amy, right? I've seen you with her and I see how much love you have in you. It leaks out. No, gushes. It gushes out of you. There's this kind of golden light around you. I see it. Other people can't, or they don't try."

He took a breath. Melissa stared at him then turned and looked through the windshield. She could guess what he would say next, but she still dug her fingernails into her legs when he said it.

"Amy needs a father," Chris said earnestly.

"She has one," Melissa said immediately.

"Yeah, but. I mean a real one."

She turned again to face him, so sharply that he jumped slightly in his seat.

"Aaron is real. He's Amy's father."

"He's in prison," Chris persisted. "And besides..."

"And besides what?"

"I mean, do you really want him around? Didn't he throw a bottle at your head or..."

"He did a lot of shit, yeah," Melissa confirmed. "But I don't ask him for anything or expect him to do anything. And there's Danny."

"Right, Danny," Chris said, and she could practically hear his eyes rolling.

"Think you're better than them?" she asked right away.

Chris shook his head. "No. I mean yes. I mean." He took a breath, trying to get a hold of the point he was trying to make. "I'm not better than them in terms of, y'know, upbringing or anything like that. Or money, or whatever. But. I'm better all the same."

"How?"

"Just am," he replied matter-of-factly.

"Are you better than me?" she asked.

He opened his mouth, then closed it again, brushing his head slowly from side to side.

"Why do you think you're right for me? What can you offer that they can't?" she asked.

"I'll be there," he said right away, as though he'd memorized it. "I'll be there, and I'll always see you. I see you now and I see the golden light of love all around and I wanna help you, Melissa. I wanna help you see that light for yourself. Since Sandy, I've seen things differently. The way people help each other now. The way they came out of the woodwork to help each other out. Even from out of state. One group came up all the way from Mississippi to help us clear debris out of our backyard. Imagine that. Imagine people doing that kind of thing for each other, all because their debt was paid more than 2,000 years ago. That's how they said it. That's why they did it. And I see that. And I hear that. And I think I have to be a part of that. Even if I can't haul wood or swing a hammer that well, I have to do what I can for whoever I can do it for. Because God doesn't make mistakes. He puts things on our path at the right time, people too. He knows where we are at all times, and he knows who's there around us that can help. I believe. I'm all in. I'm here now for you, Melissa, I'm here to—"

"Shut up," she snapped. A bewildered, almost frightened gawk opened up across Chris's face. He opened, then closed his mouth again. The budding tears in his eyes magnified by his ridiculously large glasses. "Shut the fuck up, you child," she nearly spat. "I'm not your goddamn good deed for the day. Now get the fuck out of my car."

———————

She left it behind. All of it. Her car, her bag, her phone. Especially her phone. The texts were piling up: from Danny desperate for updates, from her mother outraged that she'd had to look after Amy this long. She didn't read any of it. She didn't give a shit about how other people were feeling.

Melissa left her car in the parking lot. Inside, a band was beginning its set. Cheers, guitar riffs, and the sound of clinking glass all blended together into a grungy, disjointed chorus bidding her a thankless farewell. She crossed the bridge which spanned the bay, pausing at the center to survey the grunt of dirty lights speckled amidst the bars and boatyards below, thinning out into the tree-dark hills which towered in the distance. Further off, the New York City skyline blazed like thorns of cold dusty yellow overpowering the stars above with their muddy arms of light.

She turned and looked in the other direction, away from the city. A carpet of black as far as she could see interrupted only by the occasional red blink of a freighter's beacon far out at sea, just before the horizon. Melissa finished crossing the bridge and then climbed over the wall which ran the length of Ocean Avenue. She walked across the beach toward the nearest jetty. The small, messy waves snapped against the boulders, soaking Melissa's jeans as she made her way out. She knew that the further she went, the harder it would be to come back. She might not come back at all. One slip was all it would take to split her head open like a watermelon out there on the rocks, and there she'd lie on the sodden appendage bracketing the northern shores, the cigarette ash end of America tapering into restless waters to which her own ashes would crumble and drift and eventually sink as though she'd never existed. And that would be that. She made it to the last rock, cold and slimy with seaweed plastered across its face. She sat, her jeans rolled up as far as they would go. What if she stayed there until the tide came in? How long would that take? Would her body resist or would it simply drown? One slip, she reflected, just one. And that would be the end of this. Whatever this was.

Something caught her attention among the rocks next to her, something lodged between them, large and rectangular and splintered around the edges. Melissa was reminded of a tooth she'd had knocked out not too long ago, how it had slid across the floor trailing a kite tail of red. With her tongue, she plugged the empty cavity where the tooth had been then spit loudly into the swirling dark waters that consumed her legs. She reached over and pushed against the object, trying to dislodge it from between the rocks. The sound of it bumping against the jetty had begun to grate on her, and she was pissed about being reminded of her missing tooth and every other missing thing that had been taken or broken by some asshole who told her he loved her and would take care of her and all that meaningless shit. She pushed as hard as she could, nearly losing her balance in the process, but she steadied herself once more on the hard seat and managed to prod the board loose so that it fell into the water with a smack. One of the corners collided with her knee and she reached down to try to push it away so that it would float or sink or do whatever it would do far away from her. She shoved it with her fingertips but it hardly budged, just lapped back against her, tripping buoy-like on the light chop. The wind was picking up and the tide was coming in, she could tell. The board rose and fell again and again on the rustling surface of the water, beginning to pop and bang louder than it had when it was lodged between the rocks. Melissa tried to push it away harder, but it kept drifting back and finally, she gave up. At some point, the board had rotated, and she could begin to see, through the thin light afforded by the streetlights behind her, something stenciled in faded red block letters. Maybe "Greetings from Sea Bright"—the *real* Sea Bright, she mused. Or maybe Manasquan. Or Seaside Heights. Or Point Pleasant. Or Avon-by-the-Sea. Or Monmouth Beach. Or Asbury Park. But no, that wasn't the message it bore. Instead, the sign read, "Come in. We're open."

This is a remnant of the hurricane, she supposed. A dislocated herald of summer games on summer nights now long gone and likely never to return or be the same again even if they did. The sign had been here for a while, she could see, stained and warped around its edges, its paint battered off, its seasonal invitation scabbed by the ocean's shrill and constant abuse.

Come in. We're open.

Melissa felt it then: a rustle, a stir. She placed her hand over her stomach. "You're not going anywhere," she whispered in confidence to the night. The red light of the distant freighter had vanished beyond the horizon. For a moment, Melissa thought she had an idea where it was headed.

BACKHAND

"**T**hree Love!"

The instructor tossed the ball up and wailed it over the net.

Barry, another instructor at the club, returned the serve well enough, but the instructor knew that the match wouldn't last long. Barry played the game more in his head than on the court, a place of bodies and pulse and rhythm and sweat, which is what made him a decent teacher but ultimately a middling player at best. The instructor lobbed the ball, drawing his opponent to the net for a volley which was exactly where the instructor needed him to be. The match was over before it had really started.

Afternoon lessons would begin soon. The instructor wiped his face in his shirt, having barely broken a sweat but taking every chance to show off his abs. The students started trickling in. The boy, Max, had arrived early for his one-on-one that his parents paid exorbitant amounts for in the bizarre and misguided hope that pairing the worst student with the best instructor would improve his game. The instructor couldn't complain. Time wasted could be extremely lucrative at the club.

Max fussed with his uniform constantly, tucking then untucking his shirt from the white elastic waistband of his shorts, likely trying to figure out which made him appear slimmer. He tried brushing aside the single stubborn curl of hair, but it returned, as it always did, like a bed spring to the center of his forehead.

"All right Max, you and me today," was how the instructor began every lesson, trying in vain to coax some energy out of the boy who was more interested in spinning his racket than swinging it. "What do you say we get some air?"

Late September, the weather was still warm enough to make use of the outdoor clay courts. The boy nodded, his dangling curlicue springing up then down slinky-like.

"Both hands!" The instructor shouted as they began their warm-up rally. The boy always let go too soon. The instructor sent the balls one after the other to Max's backhand, where the boy was weakest. "Grip with both hands, don't let go." One after the other after the other. "If you don't have a backhand, you don't have a game," the instructor instructed. "If you don't strengthen your weak side, you'll never be able to stay in front of that ball." One after the other. "Your game's only as good as your worst stroke." After the other. "You've gotta be able to switch. If you can't switch, you don't have a game. If you can't switch, you can't win!" Another and another and another. "Both—hands—Max—please!"

Then, the boy delivered. With rage and release, he sent the sucker flying, clean over the fence, past the outdoor lights. The trees rustled as the ball descended into the shadows beyond the courts. The instructor watched the ball disappear, then marched past the net. He stood before the boy and put his hands to his hips, tilting his head while patting the clay with his left foot. Max refused to look up.

"What do you have to say?" the instructor asked to which the boy said nothing. "I'll say it for you then," the instructor continued. "That shit doesn't fly around here. That's not how a man behaves, much less a player."

"But—" the boy began.

The instructor put his hand out to silence him.

"Let me stop you there. Being a man has already begun. Okay? You might not feel it yet, but it's there. It's everywhere. Being a man starts everywhere. You can't get away from it. Everything you do, anyplace you do it, it all adds up."

Moments passed. The boy twisted his sneaker in the clay, burrowing a light rift in the surface.

"Anything to say?" the instructor followed.

"You're not helping," the boy said, so quietly the instructor almost missed it.

"What was that again?"

"Sorry," Max mumbled.

"You had an urge and you caved to it," the instructor said. "You wanted to do something, and you couldn't hold yourself back, and now you've acted recklessly with something that doesn't belong to you. How does that feel?"

Max didn't say anything.

"How does it feel?"

"Bad," the boy mumbled.

"Bad. It feels bad to lose control and embarrass yourself, doesn't it?"

The boy didn't reply.

The instructor crossed back to his side of the court.

"You're not helping," he heard Max say again, bolder this time. The instructor grabbed three balls from the hopper and sent them sailing over the net in rapid succession, all to the boy's backhand.

———————

In the locker room afterward, Barry patted his shoulder on the way back from the shower. The instructor stood at attention, spurring himself out of his momentary funk.

"How was the shithead today?" Barry asked, their designation of choice for Max.

"Took all my will power not to lay the little asshole out on the court," the instructor replied. "Yank that curl off his head and strangle him with it."

Barry laughed then dropped his towel and looked at his phone.

"Shit," he grumbled.

"What?"

"Just. This bitch."

Barry threw his phone into the locker where it made a resonant thud.

"What about you?"

"What about me?" the instructor returned.

"Any problems lately?"

"Everything is right as rain."

"That so?"

"That's so." He stuck up his thumbs.

"What you got?"

The instructor didn't reply, and Barry stood there considering him, still stark naked.

"You, uh, you like massages?"

"Do I like massages? Is that a question?" the instructor asked.

"You look like... Your shoulders look tense."

"You wanna rub them for me?"

"Fuck you," Barry spat. "But, uh, there's a place. Rest stop just before Exit 127 on the Parkway. You know which one?"

"I might."

"There's a Wendy's there. They have one of those massage chairs inside, next to the kids' play area. Pretty cheap and, uh, you get a good deal. You get your money's worth."

The instructor looked at him.

"You should check it out," Barry finished. He finally put on his underwear, picked up the towel, and went to drop it in the laundry bin. He paused behind the instructor, speaking over his shoulder.

"Make sure you park way down. One of the streetlights is out. That's where they go."

Barry walked away. The instructor finished getting dressed, then closed his locker door gently.

The instructor pulled off at the rest stop and slowed down as he approached the pedestrian zone outside the entrance to the Wendy's. He thought for a moment about going inside to get a cup of coffee or to pretend to look for the massage chair, but instead, he kept driving until the number of parked cars began to thin. One, however, was parked way down beneath a dark bulb. The instructor parked a few spots away and waited. Cars and trucks charged by on the other side of the bushes. A few minutes later, the girl climbed out of the passenger seat. She wore a red sweatshirt and her dark silky hair spilled over her shoulders. She crossed her arms and took a few steps back at the behest of the guy who was trying to back out. He gave the instructor a hard look as he put the car in gear, as though he were in a position to judge. When he drove away, the girl approached the instructor's car.

The instructor considered re-parking it underneath the dark bulb but decided that it didn't make any difference. He killed the engine and faced forward as the girl climbed in next to him.

"Hi," the instructor said.

"Cash up front," the girl said right away.

"How old are you?" he asked.

"Nineteen," she replied without hesitation. He guessed sixteen.

He reached for his wallet while the girl started undoing his pants.

"Wait," he said. "Stop." She did so. He could see a gasp of fear across her face and wanted to reassure her right away. "I'm not a cop," he said. She swallowed hard and seemed to relax a little.

"What's wrong?"

"What's your name," he asked, softly.

"Gia," she replied. He guessed it was made up but nodded anyway.

"Gia," he said. "Gia," he whispered. It started raining outside, light dirty drops.

"I had a girlfriend named Gina in college. Similar, right."

"Would you like…?" she began, maybe thinking he wanted her to role-play.

"No," he said right away. "Just listen."

She relaxed her left shoulder into the seat, but the instructor could tell she was still on edge and that the tips of her fingers were pressed against the door's handle as they should have been. A girl like her should always be prepared to run.

"Gina wanted to be a doctor," he went on. "She wanted to help people. Especially people in poor countries. She wanted to work for Doctors Without Borders. Do you know what they are?"

She stared at him without replying.

"Anyway, she got me into that sort of thing while we were dating. I didn't know if I wanted to be a doctor, but I was probably open to it, or to do something for other people, for people who didn't have what I had, grew up where I grew up. We went down to New Orleans a couple years after Katrina. There was a lot to do then. We volunteered at this assisted living facility for people with HIV."

The instructor could sense the girl tense up.

"Don't worry, that has nothing to do... I'm negative," he said, looking her in the eye. "And I'm tested pretty often. It's become kind of a habit. Kind of a nervous habit, I guess."

She still didn't say anything, and the instructor could tell her fingers had tightened around the handle, but he kept going.

"People lived there who couldn't live on their own for one reason or another. And we were there to, I don't know, to try to do something for them, I guess. There was this young woman there—can't remember her name. Luisa? That might have been it. She was in a wheelchair. You name it, she had it. HIV. Tetanus. Toxoplasmosis. Oh, and her fingers were falling off. Yeah, the blood wasn't circulating properly, and her fingers were black and shriveled at the ends and looked like they'd been burned to a crisp and would snap off if you applied the slightest pressure."

The instructor could hear the girl sliding back in her seat and saw her hand cup decisively around the handle. It's really unbelievably easy, the instructor realized. Just one flick of the switch and the door's locking mechanism would seal her fate, whatever that fate would be, which would be what he would decide. This far from the other cars in the lot. Her destiny would be at his discretion. How many women and girls live like this, he wondered, jumping from one edge to the next in a world of knives.

"She came up from Honduras, or Venezuela, one of those. Came up in a wave of migrant labor after the hurricane. Probably fleeing something truly horrible down there, I imagine. She had scars. Have to wonder, don't you? People don't... They probably don't give up everything and everyone and uproot and travel with nothing into a country that hates their guts. They don't go through all that for the fun of it, do they? You have to wonder: What's worse than all that? Know what I mean?"

The girl said nothing.

"So, this woman," the instructor continued. "She fell through the roof of a house she was working on. Guess that's how she ended up in the wheelchair. Maybe that's how she got tetanus too. As far as the toxoplasmosis and her fingers, don't ask me. So, she had nothing. No people, no legal status, no healthcare, nothing. One night, the head nurse at this facility asks us if we can take her to the public hospital nearby because now she has a rash that they think could be ringworm and they want to make sure it's not something else. I know, least of her worries, right? So, we call a taxi and take her to the hospital, and there are maybe a hundred people there before us and so we have to wait for hours. All afternoon and into the evening. Then it's night and people start trickling in. Let's call them unsavory types. People who've been in bar fights, their faces purple and swollen, other guys coming in handcuffed to police officers with blood stains across their shirts. And there we are, the three of us sitting there waiting to be seen. And there's a fight outside. Someone pulls a gun and there's a crack of gunfire and we all hit the floor, except of course this poor girl in the wheelchair who can barely move. So, she tries to bend down in her chair as far as she can and I think to myself, how can I get her all the way down? But I don't pull her down, I just push the chair behind a column close by and we stay there until the coast is clear and everyone gets back up and laughs it off, 'cause... New Orleans. That's how this one woman right across from us says it, just like that: "It's New Orleans." Then she continues reading some book about Barack Obama. Then finally, around maybe one or two in the morning, they finally see us, and the doctor gives this girl some ointment or something and tries speaking to her in Spanish. And then, out of nowhere, maybe she has some reaction to the ointment, I don't know, she starts screaming. At the top of her lungs. Shouting things in Spanish that I can't understand and I'm pretty sure Gina couldn't understand even though Gina spoke Spanish pretty well. Then this girl suddenly lurches forward, her face strained and turning beet red, and then just as suddenly she collapses back into her seat and is out. I was pretty sure she was dead. The doctor feels her pulse and tells us she's just unconscious, maybe just asleep. So, we go back to the facility, maybe three or four in the morning, help this poor girl to her room, and then the two of us are so wired we can't sleep. We smoke a little, but it doesn't help. We try making love, but Gina starts crying and so we... No"—he paused—"it was me. I was the one who couldn't stop crying." He took a breath, then continued. "And the next day I didn't want to see any of them. Not the residents, not the staff. Especially not that girl we had to take to the hospital. I didn't want to see or hear them. I didn't want to eat the food they prepared. I didn't want to pray or sing songs with them. Gina gets right back to it. The compassion, the care taking, the listening, the helping. But I didn't want to touch or have anything to do with any of them. Nothing at all."

The rain thickened outside. The girl remained silent. The instructor thought he could hear her heart pounding.

"I left a day or two after that. Gina stayed behind. See, I thought I had what it took to help people. I thought I had that in me at one point. But it takes something from you. And not everyone has enough to begin with to make the supply last." He paused before concluding. "Not everyone has what it takes to be a good person. When it comes right down to it."

The instructor looked at the girl who kept her eyes steady and her face controlled, trying not to betray the palpable dread that had been growing in her over the past several minutes. He took out his wallet and he could sense her relief that they were getting down to business at last. She resumed opening his pants. He stuffed a wad of cash in her hands instead.

"Don't know how much that is, exactly. Could be a couple thousand. Start small. Buy things you need first, then let those things help you buy things you want. Or just buy whatever you want."

She sat back. "So, you don't...?"

"Just go ahead."

She waited a few moments, the rain still coming down and the cars whooshing beyond the trees.

Finally, she pulled the passenger-side handle. The car light came on, accompanied by the grating ding, and she hooked one leg out the door onto the pavement.

"Wait," the instructor breathed.

Without further instruction, or the slightest indication of surprise, the girl who had said her name was Gia closed the door again, readjusted herself in the seat so that her shoulders were square as she faced him, and tied her hair back.

———————

The instructor stomped toward the Wendy's sign, mucus-yellow in the rain, and entered through the automatic sliding doors. He looked around for the massage chair which, as Barry had mentioned, was in fact next to the empty children's play area. He went over and read the sign. It didn't take dollars, only quarters. Good, he thought, because he only had loose change. He pulled out as many quarters as he could and slid them into the slot one after the other after the other. He didn't know how many he put in and he didn't care. After he'd inserted them all, he pushed the red on-button and watched as the chair rumbled into action, vibrating without passenger. The instructor sat down, then almost immediately jumped up again. He searched for the off-switch, and when he couldn't find one, he called out to the people working behind the counter at the Wendy's.

"Hey, excuse me, how do you turn this off?"

The two workers looked at him blankly.

"Hello, can you speak English? How do I turn this thing off?"

One shrugged and looked at the other who may have been the manager.

"I don't know," the woman called back.

"You don't know," the instructor returned mockingly.

"Probably just needs to run its course."

"Run its..."

The instructor turned back to the chair, buzzing and vibrating without an occupant. He kicked it, then kicked it again as hard as he could.

"Hey!" the manager shouted, echoed by the other worker behind the counter. "Hey, stop that!"

The instructor kept kicking, then started pounding the chair with his fist. Then he used his arms, pivoting to deliver the hardest, fullest blows he could with the front and back of each arm, devoting the weight of his body to every shot. He switched from one fist to the next, forward, backward, forward, backward. A small crowd of kitchen staff gathered to see what was happening. A few customers looked up from their phones to watch as the instructor assailed the chair. Others didn't pay any attention at all.

"Turn off!" the instructor yelled. "Turn off goddammit! Turn off! Turn off! Turn off!"

SWAN DRIVE

Years later it would be remembered as The Great Cattle Drive of Navesink, New Jersey. Those who lived up the hill on King's Highway had had enough. The filth, the hissing, the honking. Their lawns had become minefields of green shit. Desperate measures had to be taken. Some had put fences around their yards, others had bought dogs. All these efforts failed eventually. In the end, the geese always won. And there was no one to appeal to. Their previous owner, a horse-breeder named McLee, had kept the original gaggle in his pond at the end of the street. But McLee had died a couple of years earlier, and his children refused to take responsibility for the creatures, insisting that they belonged to the community—a word that no one would reasonably use to describe the relationships in that part of town until the misery of the geese united them. Thus, the neighborhood was stuck with the flightless tormentors. Stuck with the endless parade of polluting mayhem. Stuck with the gigantic nests wedged beside AC units which come April would be choc-full of those long Dino eggs over which the mothers would hiss with fiery tongues should anyone dare approach.

There was one possibility, of course, a sort of kill-switch option. Call Fish and Game and have the geese rounded up, shipped off, and, quite likely, gassed. No one seemed quite ready for that, though some days brought them closer to the edge than others. Still, something had to be done, and fast. One of the neighbors, a retired Navy officer named Bill Stryker who everyone called Stryker, had a stroke of genius, madness, or perhaps both. He called up a few of the houses one night and suggested that they drive the geese to another, bigger pond over on Swan Drive, which was about a mile downhill across from the school and firehouse. The neighbors couldn't imagine how they would get the entire gaggle to march all the way from one end of town to the other. The number of geese, by then, was considerable. A formidable rabble of seemingly unlimited reproductive capability and the grenade-green noodles of crap with which to demonstrate their robust plenitude. There didn't, however, seem to be any other relatively humane options. The geese had to go, and this seemed, oddly enough, the sanest option available. Not everyone in the neighborhood, though, was on board.

"It's a damn stupid idea!" Cal's father declared the evening before the momentous undertaking. "You're going to push a bunch of birds which collectively are about as intelligent as a bag of hair downhill in the middle of the night with flashlights and—what was the other tool?"

"Rakes," his son replied.

"Rakes! Oh, good God. Were the rakes Stryker's idea?"

"Of course they were. He said they were the best things to corral them with."

"I bet he did, crazy bastard. Guy either thinks he's still out on a ranch somewhere or commanding a military vessel. And those are probably his lucid days. This is a terrible idea."

"He's bringing rakes and a wire fence. First, we'll push them all into his yard, then he'll get the fence around them, then each of us will get our own rake. Around midnight he'll roll up the fence and we'll push them all downhill to the new pond."

"Why so late?"

"Less cars on the road."

"Fewer," Cal's father said.

"What?"

"Fewer cars on the road, Cal, don't they teach you anything at school?"

Cal shrugged.

His father sighed. "Makes sense. About the only thing about this stupid idea that does. Doesn't seem right. Those things, they're annoying as hell but they're not hurting anybody. I know your mom and your sister don't like going in the yard much these days. Take two steps and you step in some shit—sorry, uh." He looked at his son. "You'll be eleven in a few months. You can hear the word 'shit.'" He gave Cal a nudge. "I don't know," he continued. "Do what you gotta do, I guess. Think your mom's gonna have regrets, though."

"Why's that?" Cal asked.

"She loves those things, even if she won't admit it. Especially the one with that sorta scar on its face."

"Teardrop," Cal said.

"Yeah, that's the one. She loves it. Remember what happened last spring? When one of the nests was abandoned and something took all the eggs except one. And we brought that one inside and kept it under a heat lamp just to see what would happen. Remember what happened?"

"It hatched," Cal remembered.

"That's right, and we took that gosling outside and put it in the yard a few feet off from where the others were milling around and stepped away. You might not know this, but at first, none of the geese took notice of this little orphan except that one that we call Teardrop. She just appeared and took charge of the little thing right then and there. So, yeah," he continued, "your mom was enchanted—I mean, really, she *loves* those creatures! Which is another reason why this is a damn—stupid—idea!"

"She wants you to help out," Cal said.

"I'm sure she does."

"Will you?"

His father shook his head.

"Why not?" Cal asked. "Everyone's gonna do it together, it'll be—"

"It's a stupid idea," his father said simply, shaking his head at the ground. "It's like…" He didn't finish but instead shook his head faster, almost violently.

"Like what?" Cal pressed.

"Well, it's not a one-to-one I suppose, but"—His father closed his eyes then quickly opened them again—"You remember. When Grandpa was alive. He had, oh, how should I say it?"

"He got confused," Cal offered, which seemed agreeable enough to his father.

"He was in the Navy like Stryker. And he was confused a lot after the war. Drinking didn't help much. When your Uncle Jason and I were kids, we were out one day playing near the dock, horsing around with one of the dinghies. We hear something. Or Jason hears it, and he yells over to me, and I look up, and there at the end of the dock, sure thing, is a seal."

"A seal?" Cal asked in disbelief. "A real one?"

"Wasn't the first time," his father replied. "Migrating somewhere, took a wrong turn off the coast, ended up in the bay and then the river and then right there on our dock. Sitting there barking, flapping around. Big sucker."

"What'd you do?" Cal asked.

"Jason approached it. He said..."

"What?"

"You know how Jason was, he had moments of confusion too. But his were different. His were magical. He had these ideas. He believed in things. Do you know what a selkie is?"

Cal shook his head.

"Irish mythology. Or Scottish maybe, I'm not sure. They're seals that become women. They transform. By shedding their skins, like snakes do. And young men who find them, who want to marry them, they have to keep their skins hidden away somewhere. 'Cause if the women, the human selkies, find them again they'll have to return to sea. Anyway so..."

"That was one of them?" Cal asked, his eyes wide. "A selkie on the dock."

"Okay, well that's maybe what Jason *thought*. The imagination he had. He might have thought that, maybe. Or at least that's how I understood it later on. After..."

"After what?" Cal asked, becoming anxious.

"Well," his father began, becoming slightly reluctant. "You know I said about my father, his confusion, his drinking..."

"Dad, what happened to her?" Cal nearly shouted.

His father took a deep breath and rubbed his eyes. He was clearly exhausted, having just finished a double shift, and he seldom slept well on the road. The truck was still parked in their driveway. In the past, Cal liked to climb up into the cab and practice pushing the gearshift when his father wasn't looking, but lately the sight of the truck and the thought of his dad sitting in one place and staring at the highway for hours on end filled Cal with a sadness he himself could hardly understand. In moments like that, Cal thought he could understand

Jason better than he ever had while his uncle was still alive. His father continued. "As Jason was approaching, and the seal didn't appear to be ready to jump back into the water just then, my father came out onto the lawn and…"

"And?"

"He shot it, Cal. My father brought out his hunting rifle and he shot it from the lawn."

Cal didn't say anything for several seconds. "Why?"

"He was confused, Cal."

"But why?"

"He was sick," his father replied, his voice hardening. "He was sick, and he saw something he didn't particularly like and so he shot at it."

"Did it die?" Cal asked.

His father didn't answer.

"Dad?"

"We couldn't be sure. But it must have."

"Maybe he missed."

"There was too much blood, son," his father said soberly.

"But," Cal started, his mind racing. "Blood. But no body?"

His father took a deep breath and let it out slowly. "Not that we saw. It probably dived out of panic and then, well I'm sure the current took it down river. Or something bigger got to it in the bay."

"Like a shark?" Cal asked.

"Not unheard of," his father replied. "I don't know," he said gravely. "I just don't know. But see it's when I hear about things like this cattle drive. Of old timers like Stryker getting these ideas, playing out these fantasies against helpless creatures. It just seems…" He didn't finish.

"What about Uncle Jason?" Cal asked eventually.

"What about him?"

"You said he thought it was a selkie. Something—*someone* he could marry." Cal's father just looked at him. "So, what did he do when your dad shot it?"

His father didn't say anything for almost a minute and Cal was afraid he'd said something wrong.

"We took out one of my dad's boats from the dock that night. The Whaler. We went looking for her—it! We went looking for *it*!" he corrected. "Jason was convinced—couldn't talk him out of it—that there was some beautiful woman lying wounded on one of those little islands in the river. I tried to, but in the end, I just went with him. Of course, geniuses that we were, we hadn't thought about the tides, and at one point we must have gone outside the channel just far enough that our motor hit up against a sandbar and we got stuck. After we'd taken turns calling each other 'idiots' and 'assholes,' we decided to try and actually do something productive like signal for help. Luckily, we had our flashlight along. We took turns making the SOS signal for over an hour until someone came and got us. And even then, Jason wanted to keep looking. Insisted that she was waiting for him to save her. Kept insisting..." His father didn't say more, and Cal knew that enough had been said. His father didn't like talking about his brother more than he needed to. It was six years since Jason had put a bullet through the back of his head.

"It's not right," his father concluded, and that was all there was to say.

———

The geese had never been as loud as they were when crammed together within Stryker's flimsy roll-out pen. The neighbors circled around them, most wearing dark clothes to match the occasion, though the noise of the geese defied any notion that this would amount to a clandestine endeavor. Stryker emerged from his shed with an armful of rakes which he distributed among the group like a commander arming his troops.

"All right folks," he said. "I'm gonna open up the pen now. Chances are they won't make a dash for it. Chances are they'll just stand around until we get them going. Wendy and Ally, you two will be at the back making sure there are no stragglers. Betsy, I want you to get the car ready to come get us at the pond. The rest of you I want at the flank. Keep to their sides. Show them boundaries. Make them feel like there's nowhere else they can go except in a straight line, a single column. Try to keep them as straight as possible. Use the rakes as sparingly and gently as you can; try not to excite them. But be directive, show them who's boss. Let them know that there is only one direction to go this night. If any get loose, remember how to pin them like I showed you: one arm around the breast, the other over the wings. Think of it like handling an angry basket of laundry. Don't yank 'em. I'll be in front. Think of me as Mother Goose for one night and one night only. All right, folks, I'll open up the pen, and let's get this over with."

Stryker opened the pen. Sure enough, the geese did nothing except mill idly around until Wendy and Stryker squeezed in and began prodding them toward the opening where the rest were waiting to contain the hapless troupe into as straight and uniform a column as possible. In this way, they successfully guided the rambling, babbling troupe off the grass and onto the street. They rounded the corner onto King's Highway, more smoothly than most had expected, so much so that a fresh spirit of confidence and collective assuredness elevated the group. Any ethical dilemmas about whether this was the right thing to do for the geese, or the residents of Swan Drive who had most certainly not been included in the planning (to say nothing of the tenuous legality of the whole thing), quickly subsided as the thrill of how plausibly this could be executed overtook the band of amateur conspirators. But then, as they approached the first intersection, to their surprise and incredible dismay, the road was much busier than anticipated. Several motorists had to swerve around at a wide berth to avoid friend and fowl alike, several honking in protest and bewilderment, others passing by without making a sound, all slowing to a crawl and craning their necks as far as they'd go to study what was more than likely the strangest thing they had seen in a long, long time.

One driver came to a complete stop. He leaned out the window. "Are those McLee's geese?" he called with audible suspicion and a none-too-subtle flavor of hostility.

Wendy, Stryker's much younger wife, was closest to where the car was parked. She took a few casual strides over to the driver's side, adjusted her cap, and bent so that her hands rested on her knees. She talked to him with as much smile as she could manage while still forming words. Cal thought he saw her wiggle her hips. The others paused and swung their rakes lightly against the formation that had remained impressively cohesive but was now showing signs of spilling out into nearby yards as the momentum of the push began to slow and the confidence of its actors began to dissipate. Anxious looks were exchanged and at least one person mentioned throwing in the towel (or rake) and simply leaving the geese where they were. "Probably find their way back," Cal heard someone murmur, to which his mother shook her head and insisted that if they were going back then the geese were going to have to come with them. Others were gazing longingly down the stretch of road off of which they would eventually turn onto Swan Drive, freedom at hand. The yearning among the group was agonizingly palpable: "so close, we're so close," they must have all been thinking. Cal, like the rest, could think of nothing better to do than lightly prod a couple tentative outliers from the gaggle with the bent rusty prongs of his rake. He exchanged looks with his mother who raised her eyebrows in a show of vague, noncommittal hope. Pretty soon, they could hear Wendy's loud, mannered laugh. The knot of tension everyone shared began to slowly unwind. She gave a small wave to the meddling driver. He started his engine and drove slowly forward, eyeing everyone as he passed, unnervingly so, as though memorizing their faces. Wendy met Stryker at the front of the procession, said something brief and cheery then turned to the rest and gave a great big "let's go" heave with her right arm, at which point everyone, including the geese, galloped forward, propelled by a new surge of energy and resolve and no small amount of desperation for the strange event to be concluded once and for all.

Then, just as they were steering the gaggle onto the home stretch, a car came screeching past, blaring its horn and flashing its high beams, determined to disrupt the organized mischief. A number of the geese broke formation, spread their wings, and flap-jumped in several different directions. Wendy dropped her rake and dove after one that was waddling onto someone's lawn while everyone else ran from yard to yard with rakes wielded high in the air, chasing and corralling the creatures as best they could while trying to reduce the volume of the now frantic, anarchic escapade as goose and herder alike created a hideous ruckus on the otherwise quiet and unsuspecting street.

Stryker held his rake highest of all and applied himself to the labor of keeping the march organized and purposive. They eventually re-grouped the geese, wary of, but by now slightly apathetic toward, the one or two that were unaccounted for, and limped the remaining yards to the edge of the pond where the geese were mercifully delivered to their unsolicited Promised Land. Once there, they took to the water swiftly and volubly, gunning for the darkest, remotest corner to escape their abusers. The crew gazed out at the floating tribe and then at each other. The streetlights pulled their shadows long across the pavement like reflections in a funhouse mirror. Betsy arrived a few minutes later with a lone straggler in the backseat, her upholstery covered in gooey, yoke-like feces.

"Did you see any who got loose?" Stryker asked.

"Just one so far, up by the minister's old house," she replied.

Stryker turned to Cal. "Go see if you can find that one. Gather it up like I showed you. Wendy and I will patrol the road up ahead in case there are any others. The rest of you, stay here. If anyone comes by, I don't know, say you're fishing."

With their new and final orders of the night, Cal went off in search of the missing goose. He could hear it before he could see it, muttering atop the cellar doors at the side of the house, over which loose green shit dribbled onto the grass beneath the dark windows. He lunged, got his arm around its breast, and held it tight against his chest. He propped himself against the wall, his jeans absorbing no small amount of excrement. He sat there holding it, reluctant to bring it back to the pond just yet. He felt almost unable to move, to stand. Then he saw it: an odd shape materializing out of the darkness. Another goose was coming toward him, unwavering along its elected trajectory. As it got closer, Cal recognized which one it was. The one called Teardrop because of the scar on its face. He knew then which goose he was clutching, and for the first time in his life, watching its adoptive mother come to claim it, Cal had a sense that there was something larger going on behind the world of appearances, something far tenderer and also infinitely more terrible than he had ever conceived of.

Cal's heart jerked and thundered as he stepped onto his friend Adam's longboard, the toe of his sneaker covering the screw heads which secured the front trucks. The screws were left a little loose so as to carve better going down the hill. He gave a light push with his left foot and assumed the goofy-footed stance. The street was newly paved toward the top and the asphalt sailed beneath the wheels with a smooth rumble, a purr of acceleration. Swan Drive was a long, gradual hill that inclined slightly just past the pond which should theoretically save the rider from having to bail before the intersection.

"Go, Cal, go!" Adam screamed from up the road, perched on the protruding roots of an old tree outside his house. Cal carved easily enough at first, not gaining too much speed. The wind sang past him, and a smile curled up his face. His eyes responded to the chill rush of the air with light tears. Adam was hollering in support from behind. The quality of the street changed suddenly as the newer paved portion yielded abruptly to older, rattier concrete. The wheels rocked over the bumps; the board started to shake as Cal began to gain speed. The board swerved. Cal couldn't steady it and subsequently dove off to the side of the road. He landed with his forearms on the gravel embankment which buffered someone's newly mowed lawn, mere inches from the first stone plate of the walkway, a possible concussion averted. The board careened on, captain-less, like a body without a head, until it banged against the guardrail around the edge of the pond. Adam came charging down. "Dude, that was sick! That was awesome! You ate it! You *ate* it!"

Cal was still picking tiny pieces of stone from his forearms when they arrived at Adam's back porch. Tiny traces of blood were stitched neatly up and down the inside of each arm, both scraped pink and covered in grime. "Dude," Adam repeated, "You ate it."

"I'm okay."

The two got to the stairs leading to the back porch just as Adam's sister, Stacy, came out to talk on the phone and smoke a cigarette. When she spotted the boys, her eyes bulged.

"Hold on," she said to whoever was on the other end. "What now, huh? I guess I have to clean this up, right, that it? I have to clean you up even though I'm already late for work, is that it, huh? I'm supposed to lose my job now, is that it? Why are you spending so much time here anyway, Cal? Why don't the two of you ever hang out at your place anymore, maybe get into trouble up there?"

Cal shrugged. "You don't have to."

"Leave the skateboard outside," she commanded. "Get in here."

The kitchen counter around the sink was soon covered in damp, bloody paper towels. Stacy meticulously tried to extract every last trace of dirt and stone from the raw flesh of his inner arms. She dabbed smelly anti-inflammatory junk from a stained brown bottle, then rubbed on something equally strong smelling to prevent infection. Not satisfied, she began the mummification. Cal's arms ended up covered in gauze and small Band-Aids from top to bottom, his limbs wet and stiff and reeking of ointment.

Adam's mother, Millie, wandered in from the other room where the television was blasting one of the daytime programs that she watched every single day without exception. "What happened?"

"Nothing, Mom," Stacy said without looking up.

"Is he hurt?"

"He's fine, Mom."

Millie swept away from the scene, appearing almost to float. She lit a cigarette. She was still wearing her nightgown.

Stacy glanced at her mother smoking and rolled her eyes. "I have to go out to the porch, but you can light up wherever you want. I see how it is."

Her mother didn't reply, and Stacy didn't seem to expect her to. Cal noticed a dusty old cobweb in the high corner of the kitchen that appeared somehow connected to both the tangled white strands of Millie's hair as well as the drooping ash of her cigarette. She scratched the side of her mouth with her thumbnail. A thread of cobweb caught on a drift of air that bloused the curtain above the sink and twirled to a ghost tune all its own.

"Okay, think I got it," Stacy said, helping Cal off the kitchen counter. Adam was standing outside watching, munching on a rice cracker with peanut butter.

The phone rang. Nobody answered it.

"Don't pick it up!" Millie said urgently.

"I won't Mom, don't worry," her daughter replied. "The creditors won't know we're here." She narrowed her eyes at Cal. "Didn't answer my question before."

He looked up at her.

"Why won't you guys hang out at your place?"

Cal shrugged and looked at the floor. "I like it better here."

"I bet you do," she said.

"Skating's better."

"I bet it is," she said, nodding and squinting. Cal felt uncomfortable around her, the way he did around most people on Swan Drive these days. Especially the ones who spent their weekend afternoons raking dried goose shit out of their front yards, the way Stacy did. "Go on, get out of here," she said at last, and Cal couldn't get out of the house fast enough.

———

"You want to go to the stone church?" Adam asked as they walked along the street. There was a steep hill there that they liked to ride, but Cal shook his head.

"Then what do you want to do?" Adam asked cautiously, seldom able to predict where Cal would lead them. Once he brought them to the barn up near McLee's old property in order to peer in at the turkey vultures which were said to roost up in the hay loft. Everyone in town hated those things. They were way worse than the geese as far as Cal was concerned. The geese were only clumsy and obnoxious. Those things, when they blanketed the sky, had a way of darkening everything. And their numbers seemed to grow more rapidly than the geese's ever did. Every time Cal looked up, there were more vultures. Cal had the idea of tossing cheap firecrackers in through the hole in the roof in order to exterminate them. Set them ablaze and watch them fly out and burn one by one. Adam talked him out of it, but it wasn't easy. Something had changed in Cal since the cattle drive three months earlier. He was fearless in a way he hadn't been before, and equally reckless and at times flat-out stupid. Adam was still trying to feel out which mood had gripped his friend that afternoon.

"We're going down to the gulley," Cal declared, and Adam had his answer. The gulley was located directly behind the minister's house, whose yard was used as an access point. Everyone assumed that the house was empty and would remain that way. A long shin-high sign was propped in the front yard that read "Jesus loves me" on one side and "Jesus died for us" on the other, the letters engraved in gold that from a distance looked more like rust.

The boys passed beneath the side window, the one under which Cal had clutched the errant goose on that night that seemed at times to have taken place in another life altogether. He could see more of the house in the late afternoon light. There was moss climbing up the side wall in wide lateral stains, an infection of green. The place appeared damp and discolored and Cal struggled to imagine anything like God's love ever existing in such a decrepit place.

"Eww," Adam complained, lifting his shoe to study a green smear between the grooves.

"Goose shit," Cal confirmed. The lawn was covered with it, the white-tipped droppings blending in with the grass and weeds. The boys proceeded carefully and came to the edge of the precipice leading down to the gulley, a wooded valley-like area that stretched right to the edge of the pond. People liked to drag old undesirables there—furniture and sometimes used electronics. Some of the local teenagers built dirt bike ramps to perform BMX tricks. Lately, though, the only people who liked to go down there were the likes of Feeney (an ex-boyfriend of Stacy's known by some as "the fiend") in order to get high.

Cal and Adam peered down into the gulley. No sign of anyone.

"It's getting dark," Adam said shortly after they arrived at the bottom of the slope. Cal merely nodded. "What are we doing here, Cal?" Adam asked.

"I don't know," Cal confessed.

"Did you see something before?"

"Before when?"

"When you fell off the board?"

Cal looked at his friend but didn't say anything.

A&P plastic bags lay scattered around, lifted by the breeze like fat lazy arms. There were cheeseburger boxes and soda cups as well and an old beat-up couch with most of its yellow cushion ripped through the upholstery and its springs exposed like it had been gutted. Cal hiked over and slumped down on it. He sighed.

"What is it?" Adam asked.

"I'll be eleven soon."

"So?"

Cal looked up. "I'll never be ten again."

Adam put his finger in his nose then removed it and observed his catch. He wiped his hand on his jeans and looked through the canopy up above and at the fading sun beyond it.

Just then, they heard voices approaching through the brush.

"C'mon, Cal, c'mon!" Adam yelled then turned and charged back to the slope, clambering up as fast as he could into the minister's yard without looking back to notice that his friend had stayed put. By the time Adam realized that he was alone, Feeney and his gang had emerged into the clearing where the furniture lay. It was too late to do anything, so he turned and ran instead, hoping that Cal (for once) would be smart.

Down in the gulley, Cal crouched behind the beat-up sofa. There were three boys, including Feeney, and one girl. The girl was wearing a gray sweatshirt, and her hair was long and greasy and fell over her right eye so that you could only see half her face. The boys wore tattered baseball caps and each of them had a patchy beard that only partially obscured the craters of acne across their faces, especially Feeney's. The boys laughed a lot and the girl said nothing. Feeney withdrew a plastic bag bulky with contents, and they huddled close together. Clouds soon appeared, snaking up from the axis of their hive. They passed something around and their mood became more jovial and also more focused, alternating between shrill fits of laughter and subdued, almost hushed phases that one might mistake as communal prayer. After they stopped passing the object around, after the smoke vanished, the group disbanded and each drifted into another part of the gulley. Feeney went to take a piss while the two other boys had a cigarette. The girl came over to the couch behind which Cal hid. She didn't notice him though and sat down heavily over the springs which must have pinched her backside badly. She leaned back nonetheless and drew her knees up toward her chest. Tucking her knees beneath her sweatshirt, she appeared to rock there, the springs creaking next to Cal's head where he remained crouched and secret. Sometime later, one of the other boys approached her, unzipped his pants, and thrust his groin at her face, snickering while doing so and saying something Cal couldn't quite make out. The girl bowed her head slightly but didn't offer further protest and the boy eventually stumbled back and away. They smoked and chatted, and the sun was gone above the trees, and it was getting cold. Cal knew he'd either soon be found or would try to make a run for it. It was then that he heard the sound that was so familiar to him from his earlier misadventure: the panicked bleating of one of the geese they'd herded. This time, though, he and his neighbors weren't the culprits of the bird's grief.

Feeney emerged moments later wielding a rake high above his head that he must have found somewhere off in the trees while pissing. Was it one of the rakes they'd used that night? Was it the one Cal himself had used? He couldn't tell from where he crouched, nor could he remember the details of that night vividly enough to know whether it was even possible that one of their bizarre instruments could have ended up down here with the rest of Navesink's refuse. It did seem feasible to him, though. Perhaps he had hurled his own rake into the trees beyond the minister's house after having discovered the lone goose shivering there on the steel doors. That night was ill-formed in his mind, its chronology wet and dissolving more and more each day. There were times when Cal was convinced that none of it had happened, or if it had that it had happened to someone else and that Cal had merely acted as a kind of eavesdropper, a casual observer who partook very little in the night's events and understood them even less. Now, though, the sight of the rake brought everything back. He could feel his palms gripping the pole as they had that night when he'd discovered a new composure and confidence somewhere deep within, dragging it out bit by bit like rope, and his body had raced to house and support this new thing that was cracking forth beneath the streetlights the way that gosling had beneath the heat lamp in their basement. Yes, he could feel it. He could see it, and he could hear it once again. The hissing. The honking. The fear and wrath. What has he done to it? Cal needed to know. What has the fiend done?

Feeney was still shaking the rake above his head, holding it high with both hands like an actor in a movie about ancient Greek or Roman warriors, his laughter high-pitched.

"See what I found!" he exclaimed. "See what I found!"

"What?" one of his friends asked. The others, including the girl, had clustered around him.

"Found this next to one of those dumb-ass birds that everyone hates. It was sitting right there in the cattails."

"Sitting?" the girl asked.

"Yeah," Feeney replied. "Sitting on its nest. Fuckin' bitch hissed at me, and I chased its ass away with this rake."

"You actually got it off?" the other boy asked.

"Hell yes," Feeney replied, swinging the rake over his shoulder and posturing with his head held high like a lumberjack out of some old comic. "Sent that fucker off flying across the water."

"And its eggs?" the girl asked. Cal couldn't tell whether she was worried. Her voice, like her face, expressed nothing.

"Still there," Feeney said, swinging the rake now above his feet, then balancing the prongs on the elevated toe of his sneaker. "Don't know if she'll come back," he said, twisting the wooden pole against his palm, turning it around slowly, contemplatively. "Got her pretty good," he continued, balancing on one foot with the rake pressed against the other. "Scratched her with it pretty good. There was bloody feathers and shit."

"Bloody feathers," one of the boys said then coughed and laughed at the same time.

"Probably won't come back," Feeney concluded. "But those eggs," he considered for a moment. "Those things are driving everyone ape shit. Kids can't play in their yards. Only a matter of time before someone comes 'round to get them. Stick 'em in an oven somewhere. Pretty sure someone's already put in a call. Those assholes up the hill will foot the bill, I'm sure. We'll make sure of that. But in the meantime"—Feeney tilted his head over his shoulder—"Gotta do our part, right?"

He turned and, heaving the rake back over his shoulder, disappeared back into the trees toward the edge of the pond. The other three followed close behind. When they were out of sight, Cal stood up. He went around to the side of the couch and strained his neck so that he could see what they were doing. He could see them in a semi-circle in front of the cattails where the marsh began. They were gazing down at the nest on the ground, exposed now to the world of predators. Feeney lifted his foot and brought it down hard. Cal could hear the crack from where he stood. Feeney wiped his foot briefly somewhere in the filth then he lifted his foot again to continue.

"Hey!" Cal screamed. The four looked at him in unison, practically as one. Feeney's foot hung there above the nest. All eyes were on him, and Cal had no idea what to do.

"Holy shit, it's the mummy!" one of them said, referring to Cal's bandages.

"You're a bunch of ugly fuck-faces!" he shouted in return. Feeney lowered his foot, straightened, and squared his shoulders to face Cal.

Cal thought he could see him nodding and maybe even smiling. Then Feeney took a sudden step forward as though he was going to rush and Cal quickly stepped back and tripped over the side of the couch, falling on his ass. He crab-walked a few yards then got to his feet as quickly as he could. His temporary humiliation seemed sufficient for keeping the pack at bay. The boys were laughing at his expense and the girl was just looking at him and didn't say anything or give any indication of what she was thinking. Then Feeney began to actually come toward him. He wasn't in a hurry, though, and Cal had the sense that Feeney was genuinely impressed by Cal's bravado. But Cal didn't want the fiend's respect. He wanted his blood.

"Your mother's a whore," Cal said between clenched teeth. Feeney stopped. Whatever minor admiration he might have entertained was replaced with a grim, humorless contempt.

"What the fuck did you say to me?" Feeney asked. His friends exchanged looks behind him.

"I said your mother's a whore," Cal said, finding the words as he went, "and your father was a junkie and the world's better off now that he's dead."

Feeney stared at him. The rage was full grown in his face, but it was underscored by something else, something Cal couldn't identify but which disturbed him more than the fury.

"Come here," Feeney said eventually, then lifted the rake so that he was holding it again in both hands but this time at chest level, the posture of someone getting ready to swing. "Come here," he repeated. When Cal didn't, Feeney started toward him.

"Yo, Kyle," one of the other boys yelled. "Yo, dude he's just a dumb-ass piece of shit kid, c'mon."

Cal knew he needed to run. He knew if he pivoted right away that there was still a chance he'd escape. But he didn't move. He couldn't.

Then Feeney was right in front of him, and Cal could see the light spatter of blood at the end of the rake from the lonely battle waged and won against the goose.

"Here's your chance," Feeney said, keeping his voice low. "Here's your chance you little cocksucker to say you're sorry." Cal could see tiny beads of water dangling at Feeney's bottom eyelashes, and for a moment he actually thought he could and perhaps even should apologize. Then he looked at the ground behind where Feeney stood and noticed the thin, glossy trail that his murderous foot had dragged across the dirt. Cal stared back at him and lifted his chin and kept silent and still.

"That was your chance," Feeney said, his voice almost hissing as the goose had. "And now you're dead." He began to raise the rake over his head. Cal was pretty sure that Feeney would strike him with the wood rather than the metal but he couldn't be sure and so he braced for whatever surface was destined to collide with his flesh and bone. He didn't notice the girl approaching until her hand was on Feeney's shoulder, trying to pull him around to face her. Whether he was startled or simply furious for being interfered with, Cal couldn't know, but Feeney spun faster than Cal had yet seen him move and punted the handle of the rake directly into the girl's face. Her nose exploded in blood. She clutched her face and wailed and fell back onto the torn and dirty couch and continued to wail and curse, making sounds unlike any Cal had ever heard from a human being.

"Kyle, what the fuck!" one of the others shouted, and then both of them charged over and knelt down at the girl's side. Feeney let the rake fall and placed his hand on his forehead.

"Fuck," he breathed then put both hands to his head. "Fuck, fuck, fuck, fuck," he said again and again, as though the word could turn something back. He eventually tried to approach. The girl shot up to a sitting position, her entire face slathered in blood and snot. Cal thought he could see loose fragments of bone as well, though he might have confused this with the flecks of white that Feeney's foot had left beside the couch. She shrieked at Feeney, saying things far worse than what Cal had said, to his ears at least. Feeney's hands were at the sides of his head. It looked like he was trying to crush his own skull. Then he howled. It wasn't a scream or a sob: it was a howl. Bent over, pressing his hands into the sides of his head as far as they would go, his banshee-lament rivaled only by the girl's unrelenting damnation of everything he ever was or would be in this life. The other boys just stared at each other and not one of them looked or seemed to care about Cal. At that point, the soon-to-be eleven-year-old turned and walked all but casually away from the scene, unrecalled by the crew that only moments ago had been committed in varying degrees to his punishment. Cal climbed the hill, leaving the abomination behind. As he walked past the minister's house, something caught his attention from the side window. He turned to look. There was no one there, but Cal could have sworn he'd seen something. He went around to the back door and knocked as loudly as he could. He could still hear yelling behind him, though it seemed to be waning in intensity and perhaps sooner or later they'd decide to pursue the instigator of the mayhem after all. Cal knocked again, and again. No one answered. He tried the doorknob. It turned and the door creaked open. Cal went inside.

The downstairs was stuffy, and Cal could tell that there was likely rot beneath the floorboards. Still, the smell wasn't entirely unpleasant. The house struck him as something that was tightly sealed—like mementos wrapped in time capsules and buried deep down with the roots and stones and other unsung organs of the earth. He went from room to room. Nothing. No one. He looked out the window beneath which he'd sat with the goose all those nights ago and through which he was sure someone had looked out at him minutes before. Would the minister ever come back? Cal wondered. If not, why wouldn't he sell the place? Did he live here with someone? Did he love someone here and can't stand to be inside the house now that they're gone? And why didn't he lock the doors? Was he waiting for someone to come back? Was he secretly hoping that someone would break in and burn the place down so he wouldn't have to get rid of it himself? How many questions there were to ask about an empty house at the center of town? Cal went to the bottom of the staircase.

"Come out," he shouted into the emptiness. "If you're in here, come out." There was only silence. Cal sat on the bottom stair and looked through the murky glass of the front door. He could just make out the sign on the lawn that had been an object of ridicule and even some disdain for as long as Cal could remember, the one bearing dual notions of our debt to Jesus. He heard voices to his right and realized that Feeney and his friends were following him after all. Cal went to the window and looked out. The girl's arm was around the shoulders of the boy who'd bothered her before. Feeney was ahead of them, but it seemed less like he was leading and more like he was keeping his distance. Cal could tell they were looking for him. For the sake of maintaining their friendship, they would need him to suffer for the trouble he'd caused. Bad guys are in short supply these days, and nobody likes looking in the mirror. They wouldn't find him, though. Not now anyway. Soon they were gone again, and Cal stayed at the window and looked out at the cars as they drove past Swan Drive, climbing the hill toward where his parents were surely waiting and more than likely starting to worry, especially if Adam had called them after scampering out of the gulley. Cal remained there, solemnly watching life carry on along the main road through town. The sun set and the evening unfurled its shadows along the streets, covering people's yards and houses inch by inch. Porch lights came on followed by the streetlights in synchronized succession, brandishing their meager light against the coming night like weathered sentries preparing to plunge into battle in some far reach of the world. There was a sad grayness to it all, it seemed to Cal, as well as a quiet beauty that was, in fact, no beauty at all. It became increasingly difficult to imagine other people behind the doors and windows of the surrounding houses. Were they really in there? he wondered. He could hardly feel himself in the world in any real way and he had the sense that the feeling was mutual. After a while, he sat down against the wall and studied the apparent nothingness of the house as closely as he could. He became increasingly aware that the only thing adding substance now was him: his breath, his sweat, his heartbeat. There was nothing else happening. The house was him and him alone.

Soon it was completely dark. The only light came from the occasional wash of refracted headlights across the ceiling. He heard their voices eventually. His father and mother, Stacy and Adam. They went to the gulley, passing within yards of where Cal was sitting. They went down the hill and Cal could hear them calling as loudly as they could, their voices echoing across the pond, his name the night's defining syllable. What about the eggs? he asked himself stupidly. Will they find them and bring them home? Of course, they won't. The geese are the last thing they're thinking of right now. Those eggs are done for, prey to a fox or raccoon unless the mother goes back after all. Will she? Can she? Is it possible for any creature, large or small, smart or dumb, to pick up the pieces of what has been broken and carry on as though it doesn't matter? Cal started to resent his own thoughts and tried to clear them from his mind. His parents and the rest came back up the hill and continued shouting his name. No one thought to check the house and why would they? Soon they were gone again, and his name became a distant echo. There were lighting bugs blinking on and off, tracing dusty yellow trails above the lawn, and little else. Eventually, he lay on his side and before long he was asleep. He dreamed that night of many things, but when he woke the next morning, he could only remember fragments: blood and feathers and huge shapes appearing before him in the darkness, looming over him like a thousand shadows sewn into a single towering presence. A power he could not name or fathom, set either to cradle or destroy.

He looked out the window. Everything was still and silent. He could see the grass glistening with webs of dew beneath the light of day that was just beginning to make itself known in the sky, unstitching the shadows between the trees and houses. How long had his parents searched for him? he wondered. He hoped they had at least gotten some sleep and knew that he was okay. He wondered if deep down people knew things about those they loved without knowing how or why. Cal looked once more at the empty rooms of the house then he went out through the back door and stepped onto the cold, damp lawn. Birds were singing and the world seemed quiet and peaceful and so removed from itself. Cal felt then like he knew it in a way no one else could. The world and the town that it contained was something to him now that it could not possibly ever be to anyone else. He approached the street and looked both ways along the sidewalk. Yes, this is mine, he concluded to himself. They will take many things in time, but they will not, they cannot take this. Cal could smell salt water in the air. The river was pulsing nearby. The same river where the bones of either a mythical creature or else a lonely orphan cast from the ocean's mysteries lay entombed somewhere deep down in the silt and mud. Bones that honored both a raving old man as well as his romantic, doomed son. Cal turned his feet in the direction of his house and began to walk. They'll be angry, he knew, thinking of his parents, but the love will exceed the anger and the anger will be only its temporary expression. Love and anger were the twin engines of the world, and there was no real need for contest between adoration and terror. Both had shapes that appeared in the night and in the heart that were impossible to measure or fill. Such were the realizations he would arrive at in due time. But right then, more than anything, Cal was hungry and so damn tired, and he looked forward to being someplace once more that he understood. So Cal walked.

The sun was visible now in the sky, he could tell, new and skinless above the earth. He knew that the sun would be beautiful, but he did not turn around to look. Because Cal knew that the sun would be beautiful, he did not turn around to look.

THE TUNNEL

"I had the dream again," Philip tells his therapist.

"The one about the tunnel?" she asks.

"Yes," Philip confirms, "about the tunnel." He pauses, waiting for her to say something and when she doesn't, he continues. "It just seems so obvious."

"What does?

"The dream."

"How so?"

"Aren't dreams about racing through tunnels... doesn't everyone have those?"

Philip's eyes turn to the screensaver on her computer. Bubbles. Why would someone have bubbles as their screen saver during a paid session?

"Does it matter?" she asks.

"Does what matter?

"Does it matter that other people might also have dreams about tunnels? And even if they did, wouldn't you rather focus on what it means for you?"

"What does it mean for me?"

"What does it mean for you?" she parrots.

Philip sits back on the couch. "I'm running," he starts to explain.

"Go on," she encourages.

"I'm running through this tunnel, and I know I haven't been in there for very long. But I feel desperate maybe."

"To get out?"

"To get through. Desperate to get to the other end."

"Does it feel claustrophobic?"

He shakes his head.

"I'm not afraid of the walls caving in if that's what you mean. It's more like if I don't get to the other end then something truly awful is going to happen."

"Do you have any idea what?" she asks.

Philip studies the floor. "It's just a feeling," he explains. "A sense that if I don't keep moving—if I don't get to that other end some-how—that something truly, truly awful is going to happen and that I'll be completely powerless to do anything about it."

"And you've had the dream before?" she asks.

"Yes," he confirms. "Several times."

"How many?"

"I couldn't say."

"Try."

"Eight," he answers, unconvinced of its accuracy.

"Eight." She nods to herself, as though it were something she could guess.

"And..."

"And?"

"And no matter how fast I run, the light at the end doesn't get any closer. And, hey, I know how that sounds."

"How does it sound?"

"Like a bad made-for-TV movie. But yes, there is a light at the end of the tunnel, and I am running as hard as I can, only I realize something."

"What do you realize?"

"That"—Philip reflects for a moment, gathering the idea—"I'm making the tunnel."

"You're making the tunnel?"

"Yeah, somehow I am."

"How exactly?" she asks, leaning forward.

"It's almost as though the harder I run the longer it gets. Like, every time I stop to catch my breath, the end seems within reach, because it *is* within reach. Maybe not more than a few hundred yards away. But then I start moving my feet, to get through it finally, and that's when it starts moving away from me. And if I stop again, same thing. It isn't really that far. But I start moving my feet and, and it's like the walls are rubber and my feet are stretching them out. That's how it feels."

"Like"—she plays with the thought before committing to it—"Almost like the tunnel is you. That is, it moves because you move. It expands or contracts based on when and how you move. Is that it?"

"Maybe," he says. "But I don't know if I'm the tunnel. In fact, I'm pretty sure it hates my guts."

"The tunnel hates your guts?"

"Yeah. It's toying with me. Or maybe not. Maybe it's really just indifferent. Maybe it does this to everyone. I'm not sure which is worse."

He checks his watch. Not much time left.

"And then there's this," he says, drawing to a close. The therapist waits patiently for him to continue. "At some point, it occurs to me to go back. Like, there's the sense that if I go back that the tunnel will hold still. That it won't expand anymore and that sooner or later I'll find my way back out the way I came in."

"Oh," she says, raising her eyebrows. "Isn't that a hopeful feeling? That there's a way out?"

"Well, it might be," he explains, "except that by the time I realize that, I've been running so long. So long that, well, I don't really know how I'd get back. Like, in theory, it's turning and going back the exact same way I came. But something in me knows it's not that simple. Something in me knows that the way I came in isn't there anymore. I mean, it's there, maybe, but I won't have it in me to retrace it. It'll take too much. I'm spent, you see. Yeah, that's the feeling; that's the truly awful part. That I could get back out probably, but that I'm just too spent, just too exhausted to try. So, I stay right where I am. I stay right there without moving forward 'cause forward keeps running away from me, and going back just doesn't seem like a legitimate option anymore. So, there I am. In the tunnel. No place else. And then, then there's the really, really terrifying part."

"What?" she asks, leaning forward, like he was analyzing her dream instead of his.

"That right then, before I shoot awake, right at the apex of the nightmare, I feel free."

"Free."

"Yeah. Like part of me is okay with being stuck. Like that's where I've always belonged."

"And that's when you wake up?"

"Yeah. That's when I wake up."

———————

As soon as he gets to the parking lot, Philip's phone rings. It's Jennifer.

"What's up, JJ?" he asks. "I'm still in Red Bank. Just got out of—"

"Vinnie didn't go to school," his wife says.

"Again?"

Philip presses his free hand over his right eye and bows his head slightly.

"Still there?" she asks.

"I'm here." He straightens. "Any ideas?"

"Out with his friends."

"You call those things friends?"

"If you were still in Red Bank... Good chances they're around there somewhere."

"Yeah, JJ," he says with irritation. "I have to be at campus soon."

"Thought you weren't teaching today?" she presses.

Philip bites his lip. "Meeting with Maxine," he explains.

"Another one?"

Philip closes his eyes. "It might be," he starts. "It could be *the* meeting."

"Oh," Jennifer says.

There is silence.

"Jennifer?" Philip asks.

"I'm here."

"I think it's a done deal," he says optimistically. "They've got the money for another tenure position, and my book's been so well-received, and the students adore me. Those who pass the final anyway." He smiles, then remembers that she can't see him.

"It's great, Philip," she says, clearly unenthused.

"Hey, are you—?" he begins but is cut off.

"I'll keep trying to get a hold of Vinnie. Maybe he'll show up at school eventually. Or if not..." she doesn't finish the thought.

"He shouldn't be with them," Philip says adamantly.

"We've talked about this," Jennifer replies. "We're not in a position to tell him who his friends—"

"They're drug addicts!" Philip nearly yells then scans the parking lot to see whether anyone overheard.

"You don't know that."

"They reek of pot every time they walk through our door!"

"That's something else. That's no big deal anymore."

"It's not just that," he continues. "They're into other things. Pills. Oxy. Christ, I wouldn't be surprised if they're sticking needles in their arms."

"Philip c'mon!" she exclaims, finally animated.

"That's what they're all into these days," Philip persists. "Wasn't like that when we were growing up, JJ. Forget about passing the bong under your dad's porch, or even doing a line once in a while at a party. No, these kids, they're in deep. From the word go. There's barely any runway anymore. All of them just take off and plunge."

Jennifer doesn't respond right away. "I'll keep trying," she says eventually, evasively. "I'll keep trying and I'll let you know."

"Jennifer..." Philip begins but his wife has hung up so Philip pockets his phone. He puffs his cheeks out and closes and then opens his eyes again. The sky is getting dark, but it hasn't started to rain yet, and Philip remains hopeful.

———

"Have a seat."

Maxine invites him into her office a little over an hour later. He smiles widely upon entry, but she doesn't engage him at first. When she finally looks at him from behind her desk, she leans her knuckles onto her table, darts her eyes at her computer screen then settles on him with a look that reminds Philip of a tax adviser weighing whether to start with the good news or the bad.

"Is everything okay," he asks immediately, and only when her look does not change does he begin to sweat. *Wasn't this supposed to be a formality*? he asks himself. *Didn't I have this in the bag*? He is in no mood to equivocate. "I thought this was a done deal," he states.

Maxine slumps into her chair and laces her fingers, propping her elbows on the table and digging the joints of her thumbs into her forehead. *This is worse than I could have imagined*, Philip realizes. *Why*? he wonders. "Why?" he asks.

Maxine lowers and folds her hands. Cocking her head slightly, she opens her mouth, then closes her eyes and appears to chuckle lightly to herself. She pivots her chair away from him and gazes absently out her window where dots of water begin to prick and slide.

"Oh Philip," she says, shaking her head. "Philip, Philip, Philip," she repeats, like beating a drum.

"Jesus, Maxine, would you tell me what this is about?" Philip demands. She turns her chair toward him again, her shoulders slouching, making her appear almost laidback.

"So, you don't know about the video?" Maxine asks, taking him in with frank and humorless eyes.

"Video?" he stammers, "What?"

"The one that's been circulating among the student body all weekend," she explains, leaning forward onto the table. "The one with you—well, it must be you, even though it doesn't show much of your face—the one with you screwing an undergrad in her apartment."

Philip opens his mouth, then closes it again. *How?* he thinks and almost says out loud but stops himself. "I…" he tries, then blinks long and slow and asks, "Have you seen it?"

Philip can tell that the stupidity of his questions is on autopilot at this point.

Maxine tilts her head and Philip sees the tremor of a suppressed smile. "No, Philip. I haven't seen it."

He looks down again, his mind racing. "Who?" he asks. "Who is making these ridiculous allegations?" He tries to sound as affronted as possible while inwardly cringing. Phony indignation doesn't suit him, and he assumes that this is apparent.

Maxine appears to play along, perhaps to humor him, perhaps vaguely hopeful that there is some substance to what he's contesting. "Vanessa Waters," she replies. "But for what it's worth, she hasn't *alleged* anything. This is as terrible for her as it is for you. Worse."

"Vanessa…" he pretends to search his memory. "Okay. She was in…"

"Revolution to Reconstruction, last semester," Maxine says right away. Philip is confident that everything they have on record about the girl is right there on Maxine's screen, perhaps underneath screensaver bubbles. "She's in her second semester," Maxine elaborates. "She's twenty years old," she says more quietly. "She'll be twenty-one in a few weeks. She looks older than she is, but then again…" She stands without finishing, crosses to the window, and looks out through the rain that is now blanketing the glass. "Fuck, Philip," she exhales, shaking her head, then closing her eyes. Philip doesn't say anything. He thinks about asking more asinine questions but is not in the mood to insult either of them.

"She's of age," he says eventually, staring at his thumbs. "She's a grown woman."

Maxine turns and leans against the windowsill, her arms crossed, staring ahead. "Someone knew where to send it," she says, almost cryptically, as though pondering the motive of a crime. "Someone knew exactly where to upload it so that it would spread like wildfire all over campus. You'll have to forgive the clichés—that's where I'm at right now. Someone sent it and it sure as hell wasn't Vanessa."

"Is she...?" Philip asks suddenly. Maxine looks at him.

"Is she what?"

Philip swallows. His throat is dry and for a moment he thinks he might feel dizzy but then the feeling subsides, and he regains his focus.

"She'll be all right," he says at last, to no one in particular, nodding to himself. "She's, she's a big girl."

"Christ, Philip, do you hear yourself?" Maxine nearly shouts. "This isn't the sixties anymore in case you hadn't noticed."

"I have," he protested.

"For a history professor, I mean." She shakes her head again and rubs her temples then presses her palms together as though to pray but instead directs the closed pyramid of her fingers toward him to drive the point home. "The country, the culture have changed. Things that people might have turned a blind eye to before they're now looking at with both eyes wide open and nobody—nobody!—looks away. Not for a microsecond. And the sheer humiliation this girl must be feeling. The betrayal!"

"It wasn't me who—"

"It came from your phone!" she erupts.

"How do you know?"

"Where else could it have come from? Was someone else there in that room filming over your shoulder?! Making a porno of that poor girl who—let's face it, let's just cut the bullshit for a second." Maxine clearly has no further use for decorum. There is genuine outrage, and genuine pity in her voice, though not for Philip. "You'll recover. Eventually. You might lose this, or that. You might be cancelled, here or there. And her? You think she'll ever be able to walk away from this? The Internet doesn't forget. People do—hell, no one can even remember what happened in the world five minutes ago—but we've outsourced our memory, so it doesn't actually matter. And this will never go away. Maybe people look for it, maybe they don't. But it'll always be there, somewhere. And it's *her face,* Philip! That's what you see the most. And, of course, nearly every other part of her." She shakes her head. "And she was just trying something out, wasn't she? Trying to be a little more daring than she usually is. Trying to live a little. Playing vixen, playing bad girl. And now her life is stamped. Did she ever want to be a CEO, or run for public office? Let's hope not. And you..."

What about me? Philip is desperate to ask.

"You'll be just fine. Sooner or later. A man is almost always allowed to get back on his feet. A woman seldom, if ever, is allowed to get up off her knees. We always hang our witches in the end, don't we?" She looks at Philip. He eventually realizes she is expecting him to answer. "Well, Mr. Early America? Don't we? Don't we always hang our witches? Aren't those ancient systems of judgment always right there, at the fore, simmering beneath the surface, waiting—just waiting, so impatiently—for any excuse to come roaring back? Any truth to that, Professor? Hmm?"

Philip's dry lips move up and down, and he is able to manage, "That's not really my area."

Moments pass, then, unbelievably, Maxine laughs. A loud, cathartic cackle. "Not your area." She sits down hard. "Not his area, oh boy. Okay." Several more moments pass, and it begins to feel as though the room has begun to stabilize, like a plane leveling out after a dramatic loss of cabin pressure, which Philip takes to mean he won't be there much longer.

"And the Board?" he asks diffidently. "Do they—?"

"Yes," Maxine says at once.

"And will it...?"

"I'm afraid so."

The rain is hurling itself against the window, the way shore rainstorms do. Throwing their full weight behind the assault. Giving everything. Holding absolutely nothing back.

"But everyone likes my book," he says meekly.

"It's a great book," Maxine confirms, then adds, charitably. "You convinced me that America is still in ruins from its first wars. Except we don't display them because we don't believe in ruins."

Philip nods. The rain covers the window like mud and Philip wishes he could stay inside his thoughts where it's safe and warm but the look from Maxine tells him what he already knows.

"There was a time, really not so long ago, when people could, or were more inclined to, separate the work from the indiscretions of whoever wrote it," she says almost consolingly, as gentle as he's ever heard her speak to a colleague. "There was a time when the membrane between a person on page and a person in flesh was somehow thick." She pauses. "That membrane is no longer there. It's gone. It's long gone. And it's probably not coming back."

And without her needing to say so, Philip stands to leave.

———————————

Philip leaves the campus, travels down Route 36, and eventually turns onto Ocean Avenue. The rain has let up slightly and the sky has lightened in the east, the clouds streaked with silver over the Atlantic. It seems to Philip that he is hitting every red light as he makes his way north, which is fine with him. Sometimes he slows as he approaches an intersection, tempting the lamps to switch from green to yellow, and is grateful when they oblige. He passes the WindMill where he had taken Vinnie for lunch not too long ago. Philip wonders whether his son ever made it to school, and, if not, where he is exactly. He regrets not looking for Vinnie in Red Bank when he was there. In retrospect, he would have rather been anywhere under the sun than where he had ended up that afternoon.

Soon he is passing through Monmouth Beach and then Sea Bright. As he approaches the bridge which will lead him away from the ocean and toward his house, Philip takes the ramp to Sandy Hook instead. The park is officially closed but there is no one at the tollbooths to tell him to turn back so he drives through and parks at one of the public beaches. The sky is getting darker again. The storm clouds have resurged, converging with the carpet of night riding close behind. The air is cold and the sand whips against his ankles as he trudges along with his hands dug into his pockets. It feels good, though. Cleansing almost. Philip stops in his tracks and screams into the wind. His throat begins to hurt almost immediately and so he desists. It doesn't bring him what he thought it would. The rage, or whatever you want to call it, is something so much larger than anything his voice could translate. He lets his hands fall to his sides as the sand pelts at him from every direction.

It's goddamned hard being a man, he thinks. *No one's supposed to say that anymore, or even think it. But it's true. It is goddamned hard being a man. The anger is a tidal force, as unfathomable and deathless as the ocean, and its sadness has no equal in nature.* He wonders again about his son, knowing full well that Vinnie never showed up at school or at home but is someplace else, someplace dingy and rundown and probably dangerous. He needs to help him but doesn't know how. He needs to have the answers, but he doesn't even begin to understand the questions. He is supposed to give his son something, but he himself has nothing more to offer, and perhaps he never did. He thinks of his own father and knows where he needs to go next.

It's a short drive from Sandy Hook to King James Nursing Home. The warm smell of flavorless food greets Philip as he enters the common area. His father, Norman, is hunched in his chair close to the main television set. By the looks of it, Norman has been able to select the programming. The other residents in the room are clustered loosely around the set and appear to have made no appeal or protest of lasting significance.

"Anything good?" Philip asks his father.

Norman says nothing and keeps his eyes on the screen, apparently not expecting anything from his entertainment except to be washed along without danger of reaching shore. A young nurse brings Norman a fruit cup and whispers something into his ear that Philip can barely understand. Her nametag reads "Maria."

"That's Consuela," Norman says after she walks away, his first verbal reaction to Philip's presence.

"I think it's Maria, Dad," Philip says.

His father looks at him for the first time since Philip arrived. He gives a long, authoritative nod. "It's Consuela," he says then turns his eyes back to the television.

"Dad," Philip says eventually, "how many were there?"

Norman puts the yellow squares of fruit on his tongue, retracting them into his mouth one by one. "How many what?" he rejoins, more alert than Philip had expected, his voice gruffer.

Philip leans forward. "When you were teaching writing at Tulane. You had students keep journals. Right? You had them write about their private lives, their romantic lives, their sex lives. You collected those and gave them feedback, right? You took it upon yourself to groom them. The women. You wanted to groom the women."

Philip waits to see if anything has registered with his father. Norman's eyes narrow briefly in what appears to be some form of contemplation but then he quickly returns them to the screen and doesn't make any comments. Philip leans closer. "How many did you sleep with?" he asks. Norman continues placing the individual pieces of fruit on his tongue until his spoon scrapes the bottom of the cup at which point he inspects it briefly before putting it down and sighing.

"I always estimated somewhere in the hundreds," Philip continues. "With your reputation. All those nights you spent away from us. I always assumed. I mean there must have been a lot, right? Like, a lot a lot."

His father remains silent, transfixed on the screen, hardly registering anything at all.

"How many?" Philip presses, putting his hand now over his father's where it rests on the food tray. Norman looks down at it, almost skeptically, it seems to Philip. "Can you give me a figure, please? Or at least a ballpark. How many young women did you *fuck*, Dad? Can you tell me please!"

Norman looks at him sharply. His face is initially stern but quickly starts to dissolve. His lip begins to tremble and his eyes well up. "Maureen," he says then, whimpering Philip's mother's name. "You think I would cheat on my Maureen?" Norman asks and the tears begin spilling down his shriveled cheeks. Philip sits upright and blinks incredulously. "Why would you...?" his father begins to ask, then breaks down further. "Maureen, Maureen," he sobs. "Why would you say that about...?"

"Dad," Philip begins, but the nurse named Maria who his father knows as Consuela approaches and says something to Norman that elicits his fervent nodding, at which point she pulls him back in his wheelchair, smiles blankly at Philip, then turns and takes him away from the common area.

———————

Outside in the parking lot, Philip calls his wife. She picks up on the second ring.

"Philip, where are—?"

"It was you," Philip interjects. "It was you, wasn't it, JJ?"

"What do you—?"

"The video. You uploaded the video. It was on my phone, and you sent it to the campus blog."

Silence on the other end. A deep inhale, then, "No. I didn't do that." Philip starts to open his mouth. "But I didn't stop him from doing it either," she finishes. Philip's lips hang open.

"Vinnie?" he says, blinking rapidly. He senses his wife nodding. Neither is particularly good at remembering that the other can't see them. "How—?"

"I found it on your phone," she explains. "Then he found me watching it. Then—"

"Stop," he pleads. "Okay. Okay. Shit. Okay."

Several moments pass during which Philip balances the heel of one foot over the toe of the other. He sways and nearly loses his balance, laughing briefly in the process.

"Are you laughing?" his wife asks sharply.

Philip straightens up, laughs a little more, then begins to weep. Jennifer breathes heavily on the other end. She does not console, but nor does she condemn.

"I'm not a man," Philip eventually peeps. "I'm not. I'm not. I'm not a man."

"Philip," Jennifer begins, "Come home. We'll talk."

"I wish I was, but I'm not," he continues.

"Philip, you're not going to make this about you," she insists. "You're not going to melt into a puddle this time and then just dribble away. No. No!" Her voice becomes louder, building to a furious pitch. "You fucking. Piece. Of. SHIT!!!"

"JJ..." Philip moans.

"Do you have any idea what—you've—done—to—ME?! US?! YOUR FAMILY?! DO YOU?!"

Philip smacks himself on the forehead repeatedly.

"What are you doing?" Jennifer asks. "Philip."

"I want to die," Philip whispers between gritted teeth. "I want to die, Jennifer, I want—"

"Shut up," she commands.

"Help—me!"

"No. Shut up."

Philip clenches his eyes and bites his lip hard, tempting the blood to break through.

"You're going to make things right. I have no idea how you're going to do that, but you are. You're going to work like hell to make our lives right again. You're going to fight like hell to make me love you again. You're going to work your ass off to earn our respect and our love again, so help you God."

"But why?" he says, pitifully. "Out of all the things to do, all the ways to get back at me?"

"It hurts, doesn't it?" she says, almost calmly. "It hurts when the ground beneath you vanishes from one moment to the next. Doesn't it?"

Moments pass. Cars roll by.

"Where's Vinnie?" Philp asks eventually. "Did he come home?"

After a moment, "No, he didn't."

"I've triggered him, haven't I? I've driven him away."

"I don't know how you want me to answer, Philip."

There is a break, then Philip says, "I know where he is."

"Where?" she asks.

"He's where they all go to shoot up," Philip declares. "They've taken him there; I know they have. He's at the hills. The ruins." He pauses briefly. "I'm going to get him. I'm going to show him the way. Somehow. I will."

"Wait, Philip, just—"

He hangs up before she can finish.

———

Philip's car winds up the hill past the twin lighthouses. He comes to a red and white gate barring his entry to the former Highlands Military Reservation that has been long since decommissioned. He leaves his car and climbs over the gate which points like a crooked finger toward Hartshorne Woods that slopes away in the other direction. Philip approaches the site of the old concrete coastal gun battery that humps up beneath a heavy layer of shrubs that had once been intended to conceal the armaments from enemy aircraft. He steps beneath the archway, both sides of which are covered in graffiti. A long cave runs the length of the reinforced concrete structure that used to house all manner of weaponry but is now closed off on either end by a chain-link fence.

This is where they come, Philip knows. Where the kids come to do hideous things to their bodies. *Why?* he wonders. *Is it magnetic? Is there something about a place once designed for killing that draws those who are bound for self-destruction?* Philip can see where the fence can be pulled up at the bottom and where, with some determination, a body can squeeze through.

"Vinnie!!" he calls through the fence. "Son, if you're in there please come out! I won't be angry! Vinnie, hey, do you hear me!! Are you there?!!"

Only his voice returns to him through the inscrutable corridor beyond the fence. Philip bends down and lifts its skirt, pulling it out as far as it will go, getting down low and ducking through, feeling its ends scratch his neck like metal thorns. He is sure that he is bleeding, but he continues anyway and is able to lumber through to the other side, leaving morsels of his skin behind in the process. Philip straightens up and begins walking, stretching out his arms like the Frankenstein monster to protect himself from whatever unseen obstructions are there waiting for him. One stumble is all it would take, one hiccup of a step, to send him onto the unforgiving end of a rusty pipe like some defeated soldier of yore twisting at the end of a long wooden pike after a battle lost. Slow, slow, step, step. Philip flails his arms around as he walks further and further down the corridor. Slow, step, step, step.

"Vinnie," he calls, becoming increasingly aggravated by the sound of his echoes. "Vinnie where are—?" His best efforts aren't good enough to prevent his foot from catching against some block or other item of debris, and he tumbles forward onto the ground, blessedly missing any protruding pipe but banging his right knee badly against whatever object had tripped him. A spasm of pain shoots through his leg. Philip screams into the darkness, rolling onto his back and cradling his knee. He props himself up against the nearest wall and blinks futilely into the darkness, his eyes purchasing hardly a glimmer of anything. Night has caved in at both ends. Philip doesn't know which end of the tunnel is closer, and right now he doesn't want to go anywhere, in either direction. Vinnie isn't here, he probably never was.

God willing, he never will be. *I am, though,* he thinks. *I have always been here.*

"Philip," he hears his wife's voice calling. "Philip, where are you?"

His throat is completely dry and for a moment he thinks nothing will come out but the weakest of croaks. He wets his lips and tries and then tries again to call out.

"Here," he says hoarsely. "I'm here."

"Philip," the voice calls from someplace outside. "Where are you?"

"I'm here," he calls, his voice splintering back to him.

"Come out," Jennifer calls to him. "Can you come out of there?"

Philip can't tell exactly where the voice is coming from. It could be from one end or the other.

"Philip," the voice comes again, "where are you?" Her voice is echoing now too, as loudly as his, though he still can't tell which side she's on. "Can you come to me? I'm here. I'm here."

"I'm here," he replies, limply, his echoes resonating with hers, the fragments drifting into one another. Dreams colliding with other dreams. Echoes answering echoes in the dark.

I'm here. I'm here. I'm here. I'm here. I'm here. I'm here. I'm here.

STATIC

The line was drawn in the sand.

"Don't come any closer than this," I warned the pack, whose sole thrill on late afternoons at the club was to piss off the lifeguards as much as humanly possible. A trio of eight-year-olds had been taking turns daring each other to run over and smack the side of the lifeguard stand where I sat and kept watch over the dwindling number of people still paddling around in the designated swimming area.

"If you cross that line," I said in the brusquest, most serious voice I could muster, "I'll have to call headquarters"—holding up my radio as proof—"and they'll call your parents over the loudspeaker, and then..." I couldn't tell whether they would call my bluff and had to entertain the notion that I might actually have to follow through on at least part of the threat. The shortest of the three, the leader apparent, nudged one of the others and they soon turned and began walking up the beach toward the club, one grinning at me while twisting his nipple in some pre-pubescent version of the middle finger.

"Little fucks," I muttered when they were out of earshot. I twirled my red whistle cord around my finger, one way and then the other. The swimming area was nearly empty, and I'd be closing it down within the hour. Suzy was due to join me but was running late. I whistled and closed my eyes behind my sunglasses. No one would know. They never did. As soon as I opened them, I caught sight of a fish washing to shore. I blew my whistle instinctively which only caused confusion among the few remaining swimmers and jumped down from my perch to charge gallantly to the water's edge to make my first and (God willing) only rescue of the summer. The seagull almost beat me to it.

"Guffaww!" I shouted as I approached, waving my arms frantically to scare away the yellow-beaked predator. It lifted back up into the air, its wings spread wide, cawing in anger and frustration at having been deprived an easy and plentiful meal. (A philosophical and/or more introspective type might reflect on the conundrum of whether it was in fact kinder or crueler to spare the fish and deprive the seagull; such a type I was not). The fish was flopping haplessly in the wet sand where it had been deposited by the surf. I hesitated at first then scooped it up with both hands, slimy and wriggling and surprisingly hefty, and tossed it like a medicine ball back into the waves. It disappeared beneath the surface and did not come back up, which I took as a promising sign. Yes, it had happened: I had saved a life and would hopefully never have to again. A slow clap commenced behind me. I turned to find Suzy with her elbow propped up on the stand that I'd leaped off moments earlier.

"You're a hero," she said, her head tilted, her teeth bright beneath her shades. My own Ray-Ban's had been discarded during my valiant launch across the sand. I squinted through the glare of the setting sun that hovered just above where she was standing, bent and picked up my sunglasses, and brushed them off, effecting a cocky, ironic swagger as though I didn't actually take what I'd just done very seriously. She waited until I was back up on the bench before climbing up. That's how we'd been trained, to make sure one guard was vigilant while the other was ascending or dismounting the stand, though very few actually observed this (or any) protocol. She pulled her long red hair off her shoulders and tied it back in a ponytail. "Anything going on, besides saving fish?" she asked.

"Nada," I replied, adoring, as I always did, every moment of our exchange. She was exceptionally good looking, and her smile was so dazzling it made you want to be alive in this world just that much more. It seemed almost preposterous how beautiful she was, not to mention brainy and athletic and just about anything and everything a person could conceivably wish to be and to be near in this life. She was also untouchable. So popular throughout high school that the word seemed completely inadequate for summing up the social power she had, not to mention the care and grace with which she wielded it. And I'd made it through three years, plus the two summers that we'd both been employed as guards at the Seahorse Cabana Club, reconciled to the grim but simple and indisputable fact that I did not, could not, and would never stand a chance with her.

"How are you?" I asked. She didn't reply and for a moment I thought I'd been too quiet. I opened my mouth to try again.

"Fine," she replied tersely. Moments passed. "You?" she asked.

"I'm good," I replied and laughed involuntarily.

"Something funny?"

"No, nothing," I said with a slight squeak and suddenly wished I were capable of kicking myself in the nuts. "What's going on up at the big pool?" I asked, the squeak just below the surface.

"Guppy practice just finished," she replied, referring to the club's swim team. "Todd's coiling up the lane lines." Suzy co-coached the team. She was especially adept with the younger kids. She had a special technique of painting her toenails different colors, then dipping them in the water as the kids coasted toward the wall. If they kept their heads under without lifting to take a breath then they'd see what color the nails were, and whoever could keep their heads under long enough to accurately report each color was declared the winner. No other coach had succeeded in getting the youngest swimmers to keep their heads down like Suzy had.

"Gonna be a good season?" I asked.

She shrugged. "They suck."

I looked at her briefly. Her eyes were trained down the beach toward a group of teenage girls strutting our way. The one in the middle wore a green bikini that she kept yanking up. I checked them out as they passed and tried my best not to show it. In unison, almost choreographically, all three girls raised their middle fingers high in the air and I feared for a moment that they were directed at me. Then I noticed a young family a little ways down the beach behind them, the woman carrying her toddler in an oversized sun hat while the father waved foolishly and shouted "Thank you" as irately as he could. I understood then who their fingers were intended for.

"Probably a parking dispute," I commented. "Parking on the side streets can lead to fist fights around here during the summer."

Suzy didn't reply and the girls soon turned up the beach and disappeared. The young family did an about-face after passing the stand and started walking back the way they came.

"Probably don't wanna leave their car wherever it is in case someone keys it," I said. Suzy still did not reply. She removed her sunglasses a moment later and pinched the bridge of her nose between her thumb and forefinger as though she had a headache.

"Everything okay?" I asked.

"Lotta sun," she replied, looking in the other direction at the retreating family, then looking forward at the ocean that was now empty of swimmers. The breeze ran its fingertips over my face, and I took my own sunglasses off and breathed it in. I looked to my left. The sky was cloudless, with New York City as clear as could be in the distance. I could see the sun reflecting off some of the tallest buildings in lower Manhattan, all of which still appeared puny to me despite no longer being overshadowed by the Twin Towers. The Towers continued to dwarf all the others, even in their absence, even in memory. I closed my eyes and tried to remember those dual black pillars of smoke slanting upward across the bay, veering left with the wind, molesting the otherwise perfect sky, those fangs rising from the new wreckage, darker than blood. I tried to resurrect the buildings in the theatre of my mind, but I couldn't quite bring them back. I opened my eyes again and had to settle for their nonexistence.

"I wonder what it's like there," I said quietly. I could tell she was now looking in the direction I was, as I hoped she would. "I mean, I know business has gone back to usual. It's been almost three years, and most days nobody even talks about it. The world is something other than what it was, but nobody really stops to think about it. Most days *I* don't think about it." I turned to her then. "Do you?"

Her green eyes held mine and something behind them left me feeling strangely unsettled, self-conscious even, like she was taking me at once not seriously enough and also way too seriously. Her eyes shifted to the city skyline and then back to the ocean. I looked back at New York, determined to finish a thought that I wasn't entirely sure why I had begun in the first place. "They must have been so convinced that they were right. I think about that sometimes. The hijackers. To go through with that. To do that to so many people—not to mention their own families. They must have had families, right? Extremists have families, don't they?"

I could feel Suzy's stare and I both loved and feared it.

I kept at it. "I mean. You must really, really, really have to be convinced that what you're doing is right. Right? That it's good. That you're the good guy. Nothing else makes sense, right? It must have been—somehow, someway—that those men on the planes thought that they were doing the right thing. That it was worth everything. That they were the heroes." I paused for a moment. "How do you get there? I mean, not that I want to know. But still. How do you get to that place?"

"You've thought a lot about this," she said, clearly disinterested.

I shrugged. "I don't know. Yeah, I guess. Just having to believe about people, like, are they really evil? I mean, they are, clearly. But. Are they? Or do they just believe evil things?"

"What's the difference?" she asked. "Between being evil and believing evil things?"

"I don't know," I replied. "Maybe there's no difference. Or maybe there is. I mean, if everyone went around acting out their beliefs, the world would be a really terrifying place. Sure, it already is. But I don't know, something holds us back, most days, doesn't it?"

"So, beliefs are inherently bad?"

"No. I don't know," I mumbled, then scrunched my lips from side to side, working out the thought. "Somebody usually loses, right?" I could see Suzy furrowing her brow. "When people believe that one thing is right—that requires something else, maybe everything else, to be wrong. So. Yeah." I chewed the inside of my cheek. "So, if you look at it that way, everyone is wrong about something. Like everyone. About everything. But, ummm. Yeah. That's it."

"Okay," she said and looked in the other direction.

"I didn't cry," I said then, surprising myself. "Did you?"

Moments passed. I didn't know how to measure them. "I cried," she said eventually.

"I tried to," I continued. "I remember going into the bathroom at school, back when it was still fresh. When a lot of people couldn't make it through a single period without breaking down. I went into the bathroom and stared at myself in the mirror and even poked myself in the eyes a few times to make it happen and nada." I began twirling the cord of my whistle again, trying my best not to whack Suzy. "Maybe because I didn't lose anybody," I said. "I knew people of course. Friends of my parents," I clarified, "but not like an uncle or a Godmother the way a lot of people did. Then again…"

"Some people don't cry," she said.

"No, but I do," I said. "I do."

"Is that a fact?" she asked.

"People forget things easily," I said.

"Do they?" she replied.

I nodded. "I think so. I mean, I still remember that day, everyone down here at the beach. Everyone together. Usually, it seems like people don't give a shit about each other much. But that day was something. People just hugging. Just pulling over to the side of the road and hugging." I scooted toward her. "Everyone looking in the same direction. When does that happen? That so many people are looking in the same direction at the same time. But now, I mean who talks about any of that anymore?"

"You do," she said.

"I guess so," I responded with a light chuckle. "But don't you think that's something, that something like that could happen and everyone could just move on so automatically. Just, going to the beach again like they always did. I wonder if people who live there feel the same way or—?"

"You should live there," she interrupted. "Thought about going to school in the city?"

"Yeah, I'm working on that," I said. "My brother's there. Took a year off to figure things out."

"Figure things out?" she said quickly, almost cutting me off.

"Y'know, hang out, party a little, try things, travel, stuff like that," I explained. "He wanted to go to NYU in the fall, but so far he's been waitlisted—"

"Hey, that sucks!" she said loudly, then whistled and waved at a couple of girls who were wading outside the lines. The girls stepped back over the seaweed-crusted rope and started playing a game where they would run away from the breakers as fast as they could before the water engulfed their feet, then run toward the ocean again as soon as it receded. It felt then like Suzy was doing something similar with me. Rushing forward then backward, over and over, but I had no idea why.

"Anyway, yeah," I picked up. "I wanna be there but I'm also trying to look off the beaten path."

"What does that mean?" she asked.

"Like, not just the name-brand schools."

"Oh," she said.

"How about you?" I asked. "Do you know—?"

"I'm going to Harvard," she said simply.

"Oh, wow!" I exclaimed.

"Ultimate name-brand school," she said.

"Yeah, but, that's awesome," I said.

I could tell the sun had disappeared behind the cabana building behind us and it would soon be time to drag the stand down. The temperature was dropping, and I wished I had my sweatshirt.

"Are you cold?" I asked her.

She put her sunglasses back on, looked at me, said, "No," then turned her gaze back out to sea.

I found myself thinking about a documentary I'd watched with my dad not long ago. *When We Were Kings* which was about Muhammad Ali when he was preparing to fight George Foreman for the heavyweight championship in Zaire. The "Rumble in the Jungle." Ali was in his early thirties and Foreman was not only younger but stronger too. By a lot. There was a shot of Foreman pounding a punching bag so hard that it left a dent in the bag so big you'd think it was hit by a car. And what does Ali do in the ring for nearly the entire match? He floats. He plays with him. He bounces off the ropes. He lets Foreman wail on him with everything he has until he starts to slow down and then Ali takes him out in the eighth. He dances and dodges and retreats until finally, knockout.

"Ben," I heard her say. She turned to me slightly. "That's your brother's name, right?"

"Yeah," I confirmed.

"He was a running back," she said, and I couldn't tell whether she was asking or stating.

"He was," I said. "All Shore. All Conference. All Everything."

She grunted. "All everything," she repeated. "You play too, right?"

"Yeah," I replied.

"Lineman?"

"Tight end. Coaches tried me on offense a few times, but I'm too skinny to give much protection. Bigger guys lay me out."

"Does it feel good?" she asked.

"Does what?"

"Being on the team?"

It didn't feel "good," I wanted to say. It was the greatest thing that had ever happened to me. I'd been too small to play Pop Warner, and I didn't start once during my freshman and sophomore years. Then during pre-season going into my junior year, while we were doing three-a-day practices under the sweltering August sun, the defense coach tried me on a half-line and drilled me until I could break through to the quarterback. The coach could tell that I could be quick if I was conditioned the right way and put my mind to it, and he didn't let up on me once all afternoon. He screamed into my ear until I got it right and by the time the first scrimmage came around, I was starting on defense. After I sacked the quarterback, I was officially varsity. I remember how the sun had looked when I left the field that day. I remember a large bird that I couldn't recognize landing somewhere beyond the stands and a feeling that I had never known landing with it. That night I wept the way I wished I had after September 11.

"Yeah," was how I eventually, inadequately, replied.

"I know from field hockey and basketball," she began, "being on a team, you'd do anything for them, right?"

"Yeah," I said, "that's exactly right."

She nodded and kept her eyes forward. I nudged my pinky finger against the side of her hand, and when she didn't readjust or move her hand away, I allowed it to settle there more snugly, skin-to-skin. I straightened my posture and took a deep breath. The light was dimming, and the shadows were lengthening along the beach, the pocket holes of sand shaded as though someone had colored them in with a sharp pencil. Just then someone called through and I thought for a moment about chucking the radio out into the water.

"Ocean, ocean, come in." It sounded like Todd, who split his time almost evenly between managing the late-shift guards and getting high with the snack bar cooks after practice.

"Yeah, Todd, what's up?" I said, needing to lift my hand from where it had cozied against Suzy's and resenting the hell out of it.

"Couple kids coming your way," he said.

"Well, that's groundbreaking," I said, looking over to see if Suzy was smiling. She wasn't.

"Don't think they belong here," Todd said. "Should probably ask them."

"Ask them?" I said, confused.

Only static came through for several seconds until the voice followed with, "You'll know them when you see them."

I took my thumb off the radio and set it aside. Moments later, two young Black boys charged past the stand toward the water. They started splashing around and I immediately looked to Suzy to share my disbelief at what I'd been asked to do, but her head was turned in the other direction and she seemed barely interested in anything that was going on around us.

Todd's voice came through again. "See them?"

I picked up the radio. "Who am I looking for?"

Static followed. "Ask them if they belong here."

"Ask who?" I pressed.

Static. "They might be guests," Todd finally conceded through the radio's distortion.

"Well, y'know that might be within the realm of universal possibilities," I replied, taking my thumb off the button, and turning to Suzy. "Did I use 'universal' correctly?"

She looked at me but didn't say anything. I thought I saw the left corner of her mouth curl as though mildly amused by what I said, but I couldn't be sure.

"Just ask them," Todd said, sounding exasperated.

"That's a negative," I replied. "I'm gonna let the boys play until we close down."

Static came through and Todd didn't say anything more. I had never done anything like that before, least of all to someone who was technically my superior. Pretty soon, a woman came down and waved the boys to come back up. They obeyed and ran up the beach. The water was empty again. We'd be closing down within minutes.

"Do you think they were brothers?" I asked Suzy then quickly felt like an idiot.

"How would I know?" she asked.

"Is it bad?"

"Is what bad?"

"That I can't tell whether they're friends or brothers?"

"I don't know, Louis," she said. And something about how she said my name made me want to cringe. "Do people think you and Ben look alike?"

"They think Ben is a lot better looking," I replied, hoping she'd take the bait.

"Yeah, he's a real stud, isn't he?" she said, and I started to feel angry. I had thought briefly about going for it, about wrapping my arm around her waist, encouraging her head to lean against my shoulder, but something now stopped me.

"What's your problem?" I said. She turned her head sharply and the look she gave me forced me to swallow hard and fidget. She looked back to the water. It was cold again and I was ready to leave.

"That was nice what you did," she said at last. "Nice not to bother those boys. They probably get that kind of thing a lot around here." I waited for her to say more but she didn't. I edged closer and nudged my finger against the side of her hand. She lifted her hand abruptly and folded it over mine. I closed my eyes tightly. I was on the field again after taking down the QB and the bird was landing once more and this time I knew exactly what it was named.

"It's not always easy to do the right thing," she continued, and I wasn't sure how or why, but her voice had changed. "Remember Blaine?" she asked, still keeping her hand over mine.

"Blaine?" I asked.

"Blaine Hamill," she elaborated.

"She uh...?"

"Yeah. She did."

"That really sucked," I said inanely.

"I went to the funeral," she said. "Her father. Guess he was really pious or something. He stood up there and talked about how she would eventually run to him in Heaven and ask for forgiveness for what she'd done. He told everyone in the church that she would apologize."

"But she didn't..." I began.

"No, she didn't," Suzy confirmed. "But she may as well have. Put that much shit into your system, only a matter of time before you choke on your own puke." She paused. "It basically *was* a suicide."

She kept her hand over mine, but I almost wished that she'd remove it.

"Really pissed me off, what he said," she continued. "You don't say that at someone's funeral. You focus on the positive. You focus on what they did. If you have to bring something up, you don't bring up that. You don't dwell on how they tried to die. You dwell on how they tried to live. Or, if you have to, you dwell on..." she didn't finish.

"We should probably go up," I said shortly after she'd stopped speaking. "It's probably about time to—"

"You two don't look alike," she said. "You're handsomer than Ben is."

Now's the chance, I told myself. Start with the waist then go up to the shoulder, then...

"Did you think nobody would find out?" she asked, and her hand became a rock.

"I don't... umm..."

"Hey, Louis," she began. "So, here's the thing. I really, really don't feel like bullshitting right now. So, we're gonna skip that, okay? We're going to skip the bullshit because I'm just not..."

I kept my mouth shut and tried to move my hand out from under hers, but she was pressing too hard.

"I was heinous," she said.

"To who?" I asked.

"To her," she answered. "To Blaine. In middle school. Even in high school a little bit."

"Suzy, I've never seen you be anything but—"

"Don't tell me I'm such a nice, wonderful person who makes people feel good. You're not going to say that right now, okay?"

"What should I say?" I asked.

She didn't reply.

"She used to hide from us in the bathroom," she continued, her eyes fixed on the surf. "She ate her lunch in the stalls so that she could avoid us, but we found her eventually and would throw wads of toilet paper at her from above and call her—I don't even want to repeat the names we called her. And the more she cried and begged us to stop the worse we'd get. And she'd plead, and she'd beg, and she'd cry. And it only made us want to hurt her more. Assure her that she'd never be loved. Never be asked out. That she was an ugly loser, a waste of space, and that might have been the gentler part. That might have been the warm-up."

All I wanted was to move my hand, but I couldn't without admitting the truth, which was that she was hurting me.

"And let's not even talk about the prank calls. And her mother in the background giggling about who Blaine was gossiping with. Her chums. Her friends. We told her to kill herself. And we told her how. We were specific. We were so..."

She didn't finish and I entertained the ardent prayer that this would soon be over.

"And then sophomore year rolls around," she pressed on, "and suddenly she's got tits. And she cuts her hair. And hey, wait a sec there's a sort of good-looking girl in there. And the scumbags notice. And she notices that they notice. And they give her things to drink. And they give her things to smoke. And they invite her to ride around with them. And she tries hash. And she tries shrooms. And she crushes pills. And she does what they want her to do when they want her to do it, 'cause it feels good not to feel like shit all the time. Sometimes that's the only real feeling. And then everyone has this new idea of her, and it's the extreme opposite of the old idea, but in some ways, it's a lot worse. Because it's addictive. Because this new her is someone she decides she *wants* to be. And then it's homecoming. And she's at that house. And they get her so fucked up that she can't walk or make a sentence. And her arms are around their shoulders. And then she's in that room. And the boys come and go. The starting players. And the ones on JV, they're not allowed in. They haven't earned it. But they stand guard, don't they? Yeah. They stand guard while their friends and maybe even their brothers take turns. They stand there next to the door to make sure that no one else goes in. And maybe they think that something's going on in there that shouldn't be going on. Maybe that occurs to some of them, but then maybe they decide it's all right. Because older, cooler, more powerful boys are telling them it's all right. Or maybe they come to that decision on their own. Because if everyone seems to think about one thing in one way then how could it possibly, *possibly* be wrong? Am I right?"

Her hand eased its grip as she gradually turned to stare at the side of my face.

"You're fucked up," I said at last, fighting tears. "You're like, I mean, for someone as hot and smart as you, you're like really really…"

The waves were starting to build, and a shirtless jogger ran by, and the wind picked up, and I wished I could attach myself to one of those things: the waves, the runner, the wind.

"And I'm…" I started to say, "I'm fuckin' outta here."

I jumped down from the stand and took my radio and my whistle and pocketed the latter and clipped the former to the rim of my shorts and prepared to go up alone. Then I remembered that I needed to drag the stand down and put the large "Closed" sign up. Let her do that by herself, I thought, but then she met me behind the stand. I turned away from her, but she got in front of me, and I wished then that I was looking at anything, *anything* except those dazzling green eyes.

"Her father said she would apologize," Suzy repeated, her face clenched. "That's what he said at her funeral. And everyone forgot. And everyone went about their lives. Except her, of course. And that's on me. And that's. On. You." She stabbed her fingernail into my chest.

Then she roped her arms around my back and leaned her mouth to my ear so that anyone passing by would have a radically false impression of what was going on between us.

"I'm not gonna stop," she seethed. "I'm not going to forget. I'll bring all of you down if it's the last thing I do. Every. Last. Mother. Fucking. One of you."

Suzy turned and hiked up the beach to the club, kicking up sand behind her as she went. I dragged the stand down and propped the sign up against it. A voice came through the radio, but I couldn't understand what it said. Then static ensued and soon there was nothing.

I looked one last time at the ocean before leaving. I saw the fish I'd thrown back in earlier. It washed onto the sand once more which surely meant that its time was up. The seagulls materialized as though out of thin air. I turned and walked away as one by one they descended.

IT HAPPENED IN MOONLIGHT

Diane waited. Her husband, Abe, was busy maneuvering their car between the trucks at the gas station. She sipped her tea inside the interstate diner where they'd stopped for lunch on their way up to the Finger Lakes and watched as he inserted the nozzle into the car, nodding at one of the truckers nearby. Filling the tank was about the extent of Abe's abilities with car maintenance, and he never missed the opportunity to make as much eye contact as possible with other men while doing so. She noticed her reflection in the window next to her. The glass made them both appear slightly surreal. Abe with his rolled-up sleeves, that thorny U of white hair matted from ear to ear, the slightly bewildered gawk that seemed to have developed naturally with age. Then there was Diane's face with her comparatively fewer wrinkles. Her own streak of white interrupted the brunette, claiming strand by strand what had once flowed dark and lush like a waterfall down to her lower back. Who were these people: these strangers in the glass, gentle, harmless, sexless, and dull? She waved the thought away. None of that mattered. Not anymore.

"Can I get you anything else, Miss?"

Diane shook her head.

"Where you folks headed?" the young, freckled waitress asked as she cleared the table, wiping around the stack of bills and quarters that was meant as her tip.

"Keuka Lake," Diane replied.

The waitress nodded. "Summer vacation?"

"We used to go up every year around this time."

"Used to?" the waitress said.

"It's usually too busy and too hot for my liking," Diane said, changing the subject. "But my husband teaches, so we can't go up in September."

"Sure I can't get you anything else?" the waitress asked again, still not claiming her tip.

"No," Diane said then looked back out the window. Abe was screwing the cap on the tank, and she knew she should go out to meet him. She sensed that the waitress was looking at him as well.

"Folks seem happy," the waitress observed. She sounded almost wistful to Diane.

Diane looked at her. "Why do you say that?"

The waitress looked at her confused, affronted even, like the question had been uncalled for.

"Can just tell about some folks," she said simply. "The happy ones from the not."

The waitress pocketed her tip and left to clean another table.

Diane looked out the window and met Abe's gaze as he stood with his arms folded over the hood of the car. He waved at her, then beckoned. She held up her index finger. Her teacup was empty and there was nothing keeping her in that booth. Still, she wasn't ready to leave. She was eager to get to the lake and also inclined to prolong the trip as much as possible. What would she do when she saw it? she wondered. What would the sight of the lake after all this time do to her? Their first trip upstate since it happened. Their first time just the two of them, alone.

Abe had come over to the window. He lifted his arms to ask, "What's going on?" She just looked at him, not replying with sound or gesture. They regarded each other that way through the glass for several beats until Diane stood and went outside to join him.

Abe shook her awake when they arrived. She hadn't expected to doze off.

"Coming?" Abe asked as he lifted the trunk door. Diane opened her own door. The lake air rushed in. The day hadn't fully drawn its curtain yet; the sun was just about to disappear. Sheets of fractured tangerine bled across the surface of the water.

Yes, Diane thought. "Yes," Diane said. "This is it. We've arrived."

Abe looked at her curiously as he unloaded their bags.

"It's the same," Diane said, the upbeat quality of her voice surprising even to her. Abe looked in the same direction. He closed his eyes and took a deep breath, nodded to himself but said nothing, then he closed the back of the car.

"If there is an afterlife," Diane said then, "it must look something like this. It must be somewhere on a lake."

Abe stopped beside the car and gave her a serious look that she did not know how to interpret or return. Instead, she looked away. Toward the lake. The only thing she cared to absorb. Diane took a deep breath and held it, and held it, and held it.

Minutes later, Diane followed her husband to the front porch of the house. Abe was standing at the doorway, bags in each hand, like he was frozen. When Diane caught up to him, her eyes followed his and met those of the two strangers inside, a woman and a man, both in their early twenties. The two couples stood on either side of the threshold, each staring at the other.

———————

After several minutes of frantic knocking at the house next door, Cliff finally opened up. The landlord looked back and forth between the two couples. He appeared confused, but Diane could sense that he knew roughly where this was headed.

"Hi," he said to all present. "What can I do you for?"

"Cliff," Diane began, "what's going on?"

Cliff rubbed his forehead. His cheeks were sagging pockets of skin. He always reminded Diane of an old, half-blind sheep dog.

"Let's see now," he kept looking back and forth. "Diane and, uh, Abe—Hi, Abe!"

"Hi Cliff," Abe replied.

"Let's see now," Cliff began again, "Diane and Abe, when did you plan to rent—?"

"Cliff, we reserved the house for the next two weeks, same as we've always done."

"Oh, sure, sure," Cliff mumbled, "for some reason. Well, wait now. There was that whole stretch of time you didn't come up here. I had to rent to others, a matter of years I think it was."

"Two," Diane said sharply. "But we rented again this year and we're here now."

"Somehow, oh Jeez," he mumbled, his cheeks turning a reddish purple. "I must have really looked at something wrong then. Didn't mean anything by it. These lovely young people here," he gestured to the couple standing in the driveway, "they just called and came right

WHAT THE STATUE THINKS

away. Saw one of my signs off the highway, wanted to know if I still had anything available."

"So you gave away our house!" Diane said loudly.

"Diane..." Abe tried.

Cliff rubbed his face. "Must've looked at something wrong. I'm sorry about it."

"Did they sign an agreement?" Diane asked.

Cliff nodded. "They did, yes."

"Well, so did we," Diane said, then looked at Abe. "Didn't we?"

Abe's eyes were pointed at the "Welcome" mat.

"Abe?" she pressed.

He looked at her. "I told Cliff we'd sign it once we got here."

"Why would you do that?"

"If I remember, his fax machine wasn't working."

"Who still uses fax machines?!" Diane exclaimed.

"I do," Cliff said quietly. "Computer keeps breaking down. Never knew how to use the damn thing anyway."

"Well, you know there's also this wonderful tradition in this country known as the United States Postal Service."

Abe shrugged. "Didn't seem necessary. I just made the call. It was a gentlemen's agreement. Right, Cliff?"

Cliff nodded eagerly. "That's right, a gentlemen's agreement!"

Minus the requisite cognition or common sense, Diane thought and sighed. Abe was looking at the mat again. He was taking this whole thing in stride, it seemed to Diane. He might not even hesitate at this point to get back in the car and drive all the way back to New Jersey tonight. Diane wondered what was behind his lapse in judgment. Making a handshake deal over the phone with someone like Cliff. What was he thinking? Or was there something to it? Was he also uncertain and afraid of being here again and eager to tie as few strings to their stay as possible? If so, then why had they actually agreed to this? She suddenly couldn't even remember which of them had suggested it. Coming here had been her initiative to begin with, all those years ago. It was near where she'd grown up and where she still had some family, but Abe had grown attached to the area as well. The lake gave them both something, something they couldn't find anyplace else. Or at least, that's how it had been. Before. Now the joy they'd once experienced felt strained and nearly strangled by the pressure to recreate it. The water and the hills were still beautiful, the small-town life still charming, but the memory would always prove more beautiful and more charming and infinitely more meaningful than the moment. So why had they come? Who had pulled the strings? And who now, of the two of them, was most desirous of their severing? "So, what does this mean?" she asked eventually.

"We'll go," a small voice said from behind. Diane and Abe turned.

"I'm McKenna, by the way," the young woman said. "This is Walter."

"Walt," the boy clarified.

"We didn't get to introduce ourselves before. There was a lot of yelling."

Diane blushed. "Sorry about that. It was a long drive, and this was all so unexpected. If Cliff won't give you your money back, we'll pay you for whatever the week costs—"

"Diane," Abe said again, "this was all a mistake. An oversight. They have much more of a right to be here now than we do."

"So, what does that mean?" Diane asked. "You and I go hunker down at the Best Western?"

Abe kept his eyes on the floor, then started in a low tentative voice, "Maybe we should just—"

"No," Diane preempted. "No."

Abe looked at her. Their eyes locked, each trying to gauge something in the other and coming up short.

Abe turned to Cliff. "Is there another house available at the moment?"

Cliff shook his head. His body swayed slightly as he did so. He might have been dozing off on his feet or wishing that he could lie down. The conversation began to feel slightly abusive.

"Stay with us," Walt contributed. Diane looked at him. McKenna kept her eyes forward, appearing not to flinch at the idea. "We'll only be here a week. You'd then have the second week all to yourself. Place is big enough, I think. It could be fun?"

Whether or not he'd intended to phrase it as a question was unclear.

Diane and Abe looked at each other once more. How many strings were still tethered to this ill-fated vacation, and who now was holding the blade?

McKenna and Walt cooked that night. It was extremely generous of them, Diane thought. Really, they should be serving *them*, seeing as how one pair of strangers were imposing far, far more than the other. But Diane was tired, and Abe was exhausted, with bags forming under his eyes and his shoulders beginning to stoop the way they did when his mind began demanding dreams.

They steamed corn that they'd bought earlier that day from a roadside stand somewhere in the backroads surrounding the lake. Walt made a salad while McKenna breaded some chicken breasts and dropped them into a sizzling pan. Diane avoided most types of meat whenever she could, chicken and especially fish being the occasional exceptions, but she was in no position to protest, and she didn't expect to eat very much this night anyway. She watched them as they prepared the meal, the couple who owed them nothing but were treating them now to everything. No, it wasn't fair. But that word had lost its place in Diane's life long ago and so what did its absence mean now, in this most trivial of circumstances, this blunder, this embarrassment, this crossing of already crooked wires?

"Smells great," Abe said.

McKenna smiled over her shoulder at him. They worked well together, Diane observed. They had a sense of how the other moved without needing to check. How much time does she need for this? How much longer until he's done with that? She imagined their love making to be like clockwork, each getting what they needed when they needed it and knowing when the other needed more.

"Doesn't it smell great?" Abe asked Diane. She looked at her husband. He'd adjusted his posture. The stoop was gone. He was trying to appear as though he still had energy. Diane wondered if he was trying to prove something to them. If so, what? And why? Diane opened her mouth to oblige his none-too-subtle prod to compliment their hosts but then she closed it again. Her eyes connected with McKenna's as she lifted the chicken onto the plates. One smiled; the other didn't.

Walt clapped his hands loudly. "Beer!" he said exuberantly. "Who's down?" He pointed his finger from Abe to Diane. Diane shook her head. Abe slowly rocked his to and fro. Walt took the unspoken cue, clapped his hands again, and grabbed a bottle from the fridge. He cracked it open with his teeth and slid it across the counter to Abe.

"Babe!" McKenna exclaimed. "That's a great way to lose a molar."

"Hasn't happened yet," he countered.

"Don't cry to me when you're whistling through a set of broken teeth," she said, trying to make the sound she'd described.

"I won't," Walt said as he passed behind her. McKenna jumped slightly and smiled, and Diane knew he'd pinched her ass.

"We also have wine," Walt said, lifting a bottle from a brown paper bag next to the sink. He gestured toward Diane. This time she nodded in the affirmative.

"A little if you don't mind."

"Coming up," he said, spinning on his heels to lift a wine glass off the drying rack. He snapped a drying towel over his shoulder and Diane could tell he had some skill behind a bar. He enjoyed being a purveyor of booze, a point man for the rowdy, the one who set the pace and called the shots in a crowded room. He poured the wine into the glass deftly, holding it high above the rim, swirling the contents then waving the glass beneath his nose. His girlfriend rolled her eyes.

"Dude. It's Yellow Tail."

He pushed the glass to Diane. "Just have to tease out the flavor." He winked. Diane dropped her eyes and smelled the wine herself then took a long sip.

"Wait, wait!" Walt called. He jogged to the fridge and grabbed two more beers. After a look from McKenna, he used an opener that had been hanging on the fridge instead of his back teeth. By now the corn was drained in the sink, its steam clouding the kitchen windows, and the meat was cooling on the plates next to their side salads and the night seemed to be settling into something none of them could have imagined as recently as an hour beforehand. Walt raised his bottle.

"To..." he searched, trying out ideas, likely discarding "friendship," settling on "the unexpected."

Everyone raised their glasses with varying degrees of enthusiasm.

"To the unexpected," they said in staggered chorus.

They clinked and drank. Diane finished her glass. She looked down at the plates and noticed something. She looked up at McKenna.

"You've put out the wrong napkins. They don't match." McKenna didn't say anything. Diane dismounted her stool and collected the folded cloths, carefully removing the silverware in the process. She balanced them in a small heap, went and opened a small cabinet door above the refrigerator, threw the napkins inside, and retrieved a new set which she then distributed beside the four plates. She placed the knives and forks back on the napkins, positioning them delicately.

"Now then," she said, "I think we're ready to eat."

McKenna smiled a hard, wide smile.

———————

Diane woke in the night. Abe was snoring lightly beside her. Walt and McKenna, after a round of protests (Abe's emphatic; Diane's tepid), had let them have the master bedroom upstairs. Old folks' privilege, she supposed. They were camped in the smaller bedroom next to the living room. Diane suspected they wanted to come and go during the night as they pleased, down to the lake or into the hot tub at the side of the house. Had they woken her, or was it something else? A dream, perhaps? No, a nightmare. The one she'd had many times before. The beach club where she and Abe used to be members. A cocktail party. Loud, laughing faces spinning into a blur. And something beneath the planks of the boardwalk close to the playground. Something hulking and ravenous, scouring the sand for food, for flesh. Some kind of monster tomcat, ready to pounce on the raucous adults and racing children alike.

Diane sat at the edge of the bed and covered her face with her hands. Abe shifted beside her. She climbed out of bed, crossed the room, and stepped out onto the terrace. The sky was clotted; there were no stars. She leaned against the railing. *If I scream*, she thought, *the water will carry it up the length and across the width of the lake. It will be everywhere and nowhere. My scream will become everyone's scream, and also no one's, not even my own.* She pressed herself against the railing. She pushed and pushed. It began to creak. She pushed harder. Could she hear it begin to splinter? What would the fall do to her? Not much from this height. She'd have to fall in the perfectly wrong way for it to do anything substantial, other than leave her wounded or, at worst, paralyzed. Still, it could be a start. She pressed harder. Nothing gave. She relented and slumped down, leaning her head against the railing. A star, after all, breaking through the knot of clouds. Many sounds. Bullfrogs and toads and crickets and other things chirping from sunken chambers all around. There were other sounds too. She looked down to the left. The lights of the hot tub were off, but its lid was drawn and its water churning. She raised herself up and moved along the terrace to adjust her view.

The man was kissing the woman's neck. McKenna ran her fingers through Walt's thick, dark hair. He moved his thumb from her chin to her lip and into her mouth. He untied her bikini top and began kissing her nipples, lightly at first, pecking, then he widened his mouth fully around them. At one point she gasped, as though slightly pained. Diane could see Walt fumbling with his trunks beneath the surface. He hoisted McKenna up slightly. She gasped again. He rocked in and out of her. She gripped the back of his neck with both hands. The groans intermingled with the giggles as they traded the role of shusher, cajoling one another periodically to keep it down. They were having fun. A great deal of it. This was theirs. This night. This life. Everything that belonged to the world belonged now also to them. Thank God someone can have it, Diane thought. Thank God for that. Thank God.

They laughed harder once they were finished. They both shushed each other and then gave up and permitted themselves a second release. The lake didn't seem to carry their laughter, at least to Diane's ears. Walt turned his head up to the terrace. Diane jumped back. She pressed herself against the sliding doors. She could still hear them murmuring and giggling. She hadn't been seen. She couldn't have been. They wouldn't be that unabashed, would they? No, she decided. She wasn't. Diane slid down against the glass. Their murmuring continued a while longer. What was it that lovers talked about? She tried to remember. There's so much of it, whatever it is. A whole lifetime that has barely happened. But they manage to pull everything out of it. Aging is the growing of silence, isn't it? she reflected. Silence between partners. Silence between friends. Silence in oneself. Cracks that start as just that: cracks. Leave them alone. Don't look. There's no need to. They're only cracks. Then over time, they're not cracks but canyons. And then eventually you can scarcely remember that there had ever been anything to bracket the void, restrict the emptiness. Where are their cracks? Diane asked herself. Walt and McKenna's. What have they only begun to glimpse? What have they quietly adjourned to ignore, to put off? What beastly feline roams beneath their floorboards? What form will it take? When will it emerge, hungry for its meal?

They murmured and giggled and then were silent. Diane crawled forward on her knees and peeked again through the railing. He was holding her. Her head was on his shoulder, and they were looking out at the lake. Before long, they stood, retrieved the clothing that was still floating, wrapped towels around themselves, and traipsed across the porch boards, directly beneath where Diane knelt, trying to keep as quiet as they could. She could hear the front door slide open, then shut. Diane propped herself against the railing once more. She put her hands to her face and then lowered them to cover her mouth. The laughter began like a coughing fit, phlegmy and abrupt. She managed to subdue it. It kept trying to come out. She kept pushing it back down. She succeeded. She kept it down. That, and the rising power of her tears.

———————————

The next morning, Abe and Diane treated McKenna and Walt to breakfast at a nearby diner. They took one car. Walt and McKenna seemed happy to save a little on gas. Diane imagined that their funds post-graduation, of which this getaway was a celebration, were drying up by the hour.

On the way home, Abe pulled off at the go-kart track. Diane rolled her eyes.

"Family tradition!" he proclaimed. "Who's game?"

"Not me," Diane said. Abe waved her away.

"How about you two?"

Walt and McKenna had already unbuckled their seatbelts.

"All right," the man with the aviator sunglasses called over the tiny motors, "press on the green peddle to accelerate, the red to brake. After you've come to a complete stop, don't get out of the kart until all the others are parked." He hawked a huge squirt of tobacco. "Okay, ready, set—"

He waved the flag and the three rolled forward. Abe was instantly in the lead. Diane watched from her picnic bench. She was grateful that the others were there to race with Abe. She had in the past, and it had always felt like such a complete waste of time. Abe was laughing. Laughing in a way Diane hadn't seen in a long, long time. He stayed in the lead for six laps, gunning to the inside of every curve. As he passed for the seventh round, he looked at Diane. Their eyes held for only a fraction of a second, but in that fleeting connection, Diane felt as though they'd noticed each other for the first time in years. It felt oddly transgressive, like staring too long at the sun.

Walt suddenly closed in. Abe tried to keep the inside advantage around the next curve, but Walt beat him to it. When they parked their cars a few minutes later, Abe in second behind Walt and McKenna at a comfortable third, Diane could see that Abe was dispirited by the upset. The harder he smiled, she knew, the worse it was. Abe clapped Walt on the shoulder. "Well, that was fun, huh?" He grinned at Diane as she let herself off the table, smoothing her skirt against the breeze. Walt put his arm around McKenna's shoulders and kissed the side of her head.

"Beginner's luck," Walt said, and McKenna hugged him around the waist and tucked her head beneath his arm.

"You know I could have owned both of you if I wanted to," McKenna said, and in that moment, Diane believed her completely.

———

The idea was to rent a boat, then take it to a restaurant up the lake for dinner the next night. Diane, Walt, and McKenna stood at the edge of the dock, peering around for a sign of Abe who appeared minutes later at the helm of the motorboat on his way back from the marina.

"Push the life jackets aside, don't mind the oar, there should be room for everyone!" he called as he drifted into the dock after shutting off the motor.

"You look good, Abe," McKenna said. "Being captain suits you." Abe smiled. He took McKenna's hand and helped her aboard. Diane remained on the dock, shielding her eyes against the setting sun.

"Need me to push off?" Walt offered, straddling the dock and port side of the boat.

"Wait," Abe warned but not fast enough to prevent Walt from giving the heave-hoe with his foot too soon, before properly securing himself.

Wobble. Wobble. Walt went in.

He surfaced right away, smacking the water and swearing. McKenna started laughing.

"Yeah, why don't I pull that smart sweet ass of yours in huh?!" Walt tried wrangling onto the boat only to lose his grip and flounder back down. She laughed harder and fell off the bench slightly, her forearm bracing against Abe's knee for support. Walt paddled past the bow to where he could easily stand. He put his hands on his hips and looked up at Diane.

"Wanna come in?" he asked.

Diane moved quickly to the edge of the dock. "Come out of there."

Walt looked confused.

"Get out of the water, now. Come here." She bent over and thrust her hands toward him.

"Diane, I'm—" Walt started to explain.

"Just give me your hand to get up out of there," Diane insisted. "Give me your hand!"

"Diane," Abe said from the boat.

Walt looked back and forth between them, then he obliged Diane by stepping toward the dock to reach up and take her hand. She guided him to the ladder and put her hand at his back as he climbed up and stood before her. He smiled courteously, then waved to the others.

"I'm fine!" Walt confirmed.

"You shouldn't worry," McKenna said, her arm still balancing on Abe's leg. "He was a first-rate swimmer all through—"

"Nobody asked you!" Diane snapped.

"Diane!" Abe reprimanded.

Diane moved past Walt and ascended the stairs back to the house.

———————

It was just past eight a.m. two days later. Diane was standing at the terrace door. It was raining. She put her fingertips to the glass and moved them along with the drops as they slid down into other drops, expanding and accelerating as they fell. She singled out two in particular. She decided one was Walt and McKenna and the other was Abe and her. The drops collided, combining to a single, larger drop, losing their individual forms, merging with others, and finally disappearing at the bottom. She tried to see Walt and McKenna in her and Abe and couldn't. She saw her and Abe in the two of them and didn't want to. She cracked open the door and reached out her hand. The air was so fresh it nearly burned. She closed it again and pressed her forehead against the pane. Abe came in from the bathroom.

"How'd you sleep?" he asked.

Terribly, she thought. *Almost always terribly.*

"Well enough," Diane said. "You?"

If I don't sleep, I won't make it through the day and one of us has to, Abe thought.

"Fine," he said.

Abe took off his glasses and wiped them with a Kleenex from his pocket.

I need to get out. I need to get out from under this.

"I thought I might go for a drive," Abe said.

I know why you won't retire. You say it's the money, but I know the reason. I know what it takes from you to remember. And to be my husband.

"Okay," Diane said.

What are we doing here? What am I missing?

"Remember that bike trail we used to do? The one that passes those waterfalls?" Abe asked.

Please don't ask me what I remember.

"Of course," Diane said.

You won't want to come. I don't want you to come.

"I thought I might drive out there," Abe said. "There's an ice cream place we used to like."

Take McKenna with you. You want her to come. She wants you to want her to come.

"Little early for ice cream, isn't it?" Diane asked.

I can't decide whether you hate me or not.

He smiled. "Not for me."

I can't decide whether I hate you or not.

"I think I'll stay," Diane said.

Abe nodded.

It might be easier if I didn't come back. It would be much harder and also much easier.

"Is there anything I can get you while I'm out?" he asked.

I keep trying to say something to you, but I don't know what and I don't know how and by now I don't even know if I want to.

"No, thanks," she said.

I can feel all the ways I am less than a man around you and I hate you for that. I hate you at times so that I can hate myself a little less.

"Are you sure?" he asked.

Please don't think I enjoy this. It's impossible to hate this more than I do.

"Think I might rest a while longer," she said.

I know that there is something I'm supposed to do and something I'm supposed to say but I seldom know what and by now I barely know how.

"Okay," Abe said. He remained standing in the doorway.

Help me, Diane. Help me, Diane. Help me, Diane. Help me, Diane.

"I love you," he said.

I love you, she thought.

"Don't forget to bring your umbrella," Diane said.

Abe nodded then turned and left the room. Diane looked back outside. The rain was getting harder. It was shredding the lake. It was obscuring everything.

Love blinds us to most things, she thought. Especially when it's gone.

Abe came into the living room to find McKenna standing at the counter with a coffee mug. The shower was running in the bathroom.

"I was thinking I'd go for a drive," Abe said.

McKenna nodded but said nothing.

"Would you like to come?" Abe asked. "Maybe stop for coffee somewhere."

McKenna glanced at the full pot behind her then answered, "Sure."

The shower stopped running.

"Should you tell him?" Abe asked.

"He's fine," McKenna replied, and they left soon after. Abe did not bring his umbrella.

The benches of the picnic table across from the ice cream shop were dark with rain. Abe and McKenna placed their coffees down and adjusted themselves on the damp seats. A group of children was seated at a table nearby wearing nice clothes, likely for church.

"How's your coffee?" he asked McKenna.

She gave a thumbs-up.

"You're leaving in a couple of days," Abe said.

McKenna nodded.

"Back to the city?" he asked.

She nodded again.

"I wish we weren't," she said.

"Why's that?"

She shrugged and looked down slightly. "Don't always feel like I belong there."

"Where do you belong?"

"Can't say. Not here and not there." She sipped her coffee and kept her eyes directed at the table. "Things got heavy there. For me."

"How do you mean?"

"Walt used to date a friend of mine. One of my best friends in college."

"Oh. And then the two of you…"

McKenna nodded. "It was bad."

"Were they still together when the two of you…?" Abe asked.

"That's a technicality," McKenna replied.

"So yes," Abe said.

"So yes," McKenna confirmed, looking up.

"Was it worth it?" Abe asked.

McKenna looked at him. "How do you mean?"

"Do you love him?"

She didn't reply right away. The children were pushing each other at the neighboring table. They started an arm-wrestling contest. One boy repeatedly lost but kept propping his arm up for more, the clean-pressed sleeve of his shirt becoming more stained each time it was slammed onto the wood.

"He wanted to ask me to marry him here," McKenna said eventually.

"How do you know?" Abe asked.

"I know," McKenna replied.

"And he won't?"

"I don't think so."

"Why not?"

McKenna finished her coffee, tilted her head back and closed her eyes then opened them again and looked up at the sky.

"He took me white water rafting before we came here," she said. "We stayed at this Bed and Breakfast. There was a river close by. We went out there at night, wandered down the bank, took off our clothes, and splashed around. The moon was out. Once we came out of the water we lay on the grass and looked up at it. We were there for a long time, just lying there looking at the moon. I thought to myself: This is when you should know. This is when it will happen. It doesn't get more perfect than this. This is when people fall in love or realize how in love they already are. This is the knowing moment. If not now, then never." She paused for a few more moments then continued. "It's not his fault. He's got everything. He gives me everything. It's not his fault." McKenna turned and lobbed her empty cup into a waste bin. "I wish I did," she added. "I keep telling myself, it won't get better than this—"

"It will," Abe interrupted.

McKenna looked at him.

"You'll know when you know," Abe assured her. "And that will be all you'll need."

"How?" McKenna asked in earnest.

Abe shook his head. "You'll look at him, whoever he is, and something will wash over you. It won't be a thought. It might not even be a feeling. But it will fill you. You'll know."

"Is that how you felt with Diane?" McKenna asked.

"Yes," Abe replied right away.

"That's clear to me."

"Is it?" Abe asked.

"Yes. Love looks at itself all the time. The way you and Diane do."

Abe laced his fingers and leaned back. The children were ready to leave, stained sleeves and all. Church, or wherever they were headed that morning, was about to begin. Abe and McKenna were soon alone in the park.

"You see it all at once," Abe observed.

"See what?" McKenna asked.

"Who they are. Who they'll become. It's all in there. Some traits are more dominant at one time or another. But it's all in there. You see who they are and how they'll be if you look closely enough. Some kids, it's like you can see the adults they're bound to become. Some boys don't even particularly look like boys. They look like men disputing with nature about height and weight. They look like, like nature is impatient for them to grow up."

McKenna moved her hands onto his.

"You lost someone," she said quietly.

Abe didn't look at her, not at first.

"You had a son," she continued. "What was his name?"

"Alvin," Abe replied, still avoiding her eyes. He spoke to her and away from her. McKenna's hands had tightened around his, her thumbs poised at his knuckles. He opened his mouth then closed it again then opened it and said, quickly, "He drowned. It happened in moonlight." That was all.

They sat there silently for several minutes. Abe eventually looked at McKenna whose eyes were sparkly with tears.

"Whatever made you was wonderful," Abe said, and McKenna appeared confused. "You were made wonderful," he elaborated then bent down and kissed her hands. He nestled over them, his face near the table's surface, his eyes adding imperceptibly to its darkness.

———————

Diane was still standing at the terrace door when Walt came in. She could see his dim reflection in the glass. He didn't announce himself and Diane allowed him to stand quietly and stare at her back.

"Diane," he said eventually.

She turned slowly. Walt came further into the room. He stood beside the bed.

"Are you...?" he began to ask.

"I'm fine," Diane said. She took a step toward him. They were less than three feet apart.

"They're out," Walt reported.

"I know," Diane replied.

Walt sat on the bed. He stared at the wall and at nothing.

"Do you think they're...?" he began.

Diane sat beside him. "Would that bother you?"

He looked at her. "I don't think we should try to own love," he said.

Diane lifted her eyebrows. "Oh."

Walt shook his head. "I think that can lead to disaster."

"How so?" she asked.

Walt shrugged. "People have it for a while if they're lucky. They share it. And then"—his eyes moved briefly to the glass door then back to Diane—"There's this pressure we all assume, that love should last.

That to experience it at one time with one person means that you should then be capable of sustaining that same love with that same person over a lifetime. Do you know what I mean?"

Diane wasn't sure how to respond but tried anyway. "I'm Abe's second wife," she said.

"Oh," Walt said, nodding to himself. "I thought that might have been the case. He's—"

"Older, yes."

"By a lot," Walt said generously.

Diane tilted her head and smiled. *Sweet boy*, she thought. "By enough."

"And you weren't married before?" Walt asked.

Diane shook her head. "Couple close calls," she explained. "But Abe was the first that I thought, 'Okay. Let's try this.'"

Walt nodded thoughtfully. "So, it was an experiment?"

"It still is," Diane said.

"And you think it's possible?" Walt asked. "To sustain what you felt over a lifetime."

Diane didn't say anything at first. She could sense Walt's eagerness to learn something.

"I'm afraid I can't offer you much guidance," she said finally. "This is all something that just goes along." They were silent for a while, then Diane continued, "One of the biggest parts of any relationship is wondering whether or not it's strong enough to survive. Marriage itself is like a child in that respect." Walt straightened his back and tilted his head. "So you test it," she elaborated. "You test it to see how much it has left. To see if it has what it takes. You test it by going out as far as you can. Sometimes you turn back. Sometimes you don't. Sometimes the partner waits. Sometimes they don't. Sometimes the bond you share surfaces, and sometimes..." Diane dropped her eyes to the comforter.

"See, that's what I mean," Walt picked up, inching closer to her. "That's how it should be. Constantly testing. Trying new things. New people." He inched closer. "There should be no one-size-fits-all. Not with something like this. People are so cynical about relationships, about marriage. They always cite the statistics. Over 50% divorce rate. Stuff like that. But, see, they're missing the point."

"What is the point?" Diane asked, looking up.

"The point is that it happened at all," Walt said. "People get so depressed about love not lasting that they miss the importance and the beauty of the fact that it could happen in the first place. Maybe it's not supposed to last. Sometimes it does. But sometimes love is practice for more love. Like Abe's first wife, probably, and whoever you were with before him. Right? Practicing for the real thing. And maybe we shouldn't even say that, because it was all real. All of it. Even the stupid stuff. That was as real as the real stuff. It has to be. It's all part of it. The beauty, the sacredness, of people wanting to be with other people, as close as humanly possible. We don't think about it that way, but we should dammit! We should."

"Love practicing love," Diane echoed.

"Right!" Walt affirmed. "Love practicing love practicing love practicing..."

He leaned forward and kissed her. Diane closed her eyes and kept them that way after he withdrew.

"Was that okay?" he asked gently.

Diane nodded, her eyes closed. *Take me away,* she thought. "Make me forget," she said.

Diane could hear the bed springs creak beneath Walt's shifting weight as he leaned toward her and kissed her again more deeply. He kissed her mouth then moved to the side of her face, up to her temple, and then across her forehead. He smelled her hair and took strands of it into his mouth. Diane could tell that he was fascinated by the white. He came back down to her mouth, kissed her again, and asked, "May I?"

Diane let him unbutton her nightgown and move his hands across her chest. She tried to imagine him and McKenna in the hot tub that night, but the imagery wasn't helping and so she opened her eyes and took in the dimensions of their encounter as completely as she could. Walt had taken off his shirt and Diane could tell that he was eager for her to see the tattoos above his abdomen. He's aspiring to a fantasy, she could tell. He wants this to be memorable.

She lay back on the pillows and Walt climbed over her and recommenced kissing her everywhere he could think to kiss. From the top of her head down to her neck then down along her sternum, her stomach, and then further down. She thought about dissuading him, but his avidness was almost impossible to resist. She allowed herself to feel him in the entirety of who he was in that moment and what he wanted to do and how he wanted to make her feel. He moved slowly, carefully, methodically. He was taking a tour. He was as curious as he was aroused. He wanted to smooth her creases. He wanted to unfold and shake her out. He wanted to marvel at the stamina of desire as it bumps up against the precipice of twilight. And she was patient; she was enabling. She was happy then to be both exhibit and idol.

He came back to her mouth eventually and soon after, he entered her. At first, she gripped the back of his neck the way she remembered McKenna had, but then instead wrapped her arms firmly around him and drew him as close to her as she could. Diane periodically shifted her eyes to the drops on the other side of the terrace door and imagined for a moment that they were all swirling upward instead of downward and that the earth and all its quiet places were returning the rain to its first and final silence. She imagined too that each drop was a fragment of her life—the was, the is, the would be—and that if she could focus on each one intensely enough, she might be able to trace all the errors back to their innocent origins and then correct their trajectory. But believing, as she did, that the will of water closely aligns with that of fate, then the direction of each drop was all but certainly irredeemable, each course fastened and unavailable to revision. And somewhere there between those drops, within the deficit between wish and result, was the simple but unshakeable resolve that defined both life and love against atrophy and decay. And somehow, impossibly, against every odd, there might yet be peace to be found. After he finished, Walt began to cry. Diane moved her hand to the side of his face, stroking it, switching roles almost automatically, as she had somehow expected she would have to.

"It's okay," she whispered into his ear as he wept against her. "Shhh. It's okay."

"I love her so much," Walt said into the sheets. "I love her so, so much."

"I know," Diane consoled. "I know you do, sweetie."

He rolled onto his back, and she curled beside him. She rubbed her hand along the side of his face and then wiped the tears it had absorbed onto her own cheek. He moved his thumb behind her ear, and they lay that way, heads close. The rain continued rattling against the roof and soon Walt was lightly snoring. Diane sat up, put her nightgown back on, and left the room.

McKenna and Abe entered the downstairs of the house.

"Diane!" Abe called. No one answered. "Diane!!" he called again more loudly.

"Walt!" McKenna followed.

They heard footsteps upstairs coming along the hallway from the bedroom. Moments later, Walt came into the living room in his underwear, pulling a t-shirt down to his waist and looking alarmed.

"Where is she?" Abe asked. "Is she still upstairs?"

Walt looked from him to McKenna who stood slightly behind Abe and whose face was blank. Walt shook his head. "She's not up there."

"Where is she?" Abe asked again.

Walt shook his head and looked at the ground. "I don't know."

"You don't...?"

"I fell asleep."

Abe let out a long sigh and went from room to room then checked the upstairs bathroom. McKenna and Walt stood staring at one another, neither yet prepared to speak.

Abe came back downstairs and went immediately to the window. He peered down to the beach, then ran back outside as the rain began picking up once again.

He charged down the stairs and raced to the edge of the dock. He called her name again and scanned the depths as best he could. He turned back to the house. McKenna and Walt were coming down the stairs now as well. He was on his way to meet them when something caught his attention at the far end of the beach. He ran as hard as he could toward the drooping awning of a downed tree leaning out over the water where his wife sat on a rock with her bare feet resting in the shallows. She didn't appear to notice Abe as he approached.

"Diane," he said. "I thought... Oh, Diane—I thought..."

She looked at him, almost mechanically detached.

Moments passed.

"I wanted to end things," she said at last.

Abe opened his mouth then closed it again then took a deep breath and said, "I know."

She didn't say anything else and turned and looked back out at the water.

"I don't want to be afraid anymore, Abe."

"Neither do I," he agreed.

"Then let's be done with it," she said with a faint smile. "Let's just be done with it."

"How?" he asked. "How are we going to do that?"

She put her hand to his face, imagining that she was passing along the tears that she'd carried over from a young man whose love for a woman was so strong it would probably tear him apart piece by piece if it hadn't already. She leaned close to him, as close as she could get.

"I'm going to find it," she whispered. "I'm going in to find it now. Here."

Abe narrowed his eyes, nodding, appearing almost amused by something. "The afterlife," he remembered. "If there is an afterlife…" He chuckled softly and shook his head, as though realizing something both startlingly obvious and supremely elusive.

"Ours is the afterlife," Diane replied. "And after our lives, we remain."

Diane stood up then and walked into the lake. Abe glanced over his shoulder. Walt and McKenna remained at a respectful distance, holding hands. Abe watched as Diane waded out several feet then began pulling herself through the water. Then, nearly halfway to the opposite shore, she dove under. The ripples fanned out, demarcating the singular gravity of her descent. Abe waited for his wife to surface once more. He waited for her to breathe. He waited.

THE SAWED RUNG

"I won't be long," Lucy told her daughter in the car. Emily nodded and looked back at her phone. "Not long" according to her mother was an extremely flexible timeframe, ranging anywhere from ten minutes to over an hour. Emily assumed it would be closer to the latter this time. Her mother always needed more time when she dropped by to see Dwayne. Maybe because of how slowly he moved in his wheelchair, or how gradually he described his week to her. Perhaps he just didn't want her to leave so soon, whether he expressly said this or not. Maybe her mom didn't want to leave so soon either, even if the two of them had broken up years ago. No matter how long it took, Emily wouldn't participate in the visit. That was where she drew the line. Emily was prepared to accompany her mother on the drive on the condition that she wouldn't have to actually come inside the house and provided that she would never again have to share the same space with Dwayne as long as she lived.

"Emily," her mother said, at which Emily looked up from her phone. "I'd like to spend some time with you afterward. Heading to college soon, who knows how many more chances you and I will..." Lucy paused, swallowed, blinked, and continued. "Would you like to go to a movie?"

Emily didn't know what to say at first. "Which one?" she asked.

Her mother shrugged. "Maybe, see what looks good when we get there?"

"I could look it up—" Emily started to suggest.

"Let's just, let's see what's there when we arrive. Y'know. Old school."

Emily eventually nodded in the affirmative which seemed to please her mother. She had suspected it would. When Lucy got out of the car and went to see Dwayne, Emily put her phone on the dashboard and reflected on their exchange. Something was up. They hadn't been to a movie together in a long time, years maybe. They used to go on a regular basis, mostly because of Lucy, for whom going to the movies seemed like more of a religious experience. She needed, probably more than most people did, routine excursions into plots and landscapes infinitely more thrilling, funny, and stable than her own. Emily, on the other hand, had little love for the movies. Ever since she was a child, the happy endings of family films seemed more tormenting than comforting.

When she was in fourth grade, the teacher showed her class the film *A Little Princess* before the start of Christmas break. At the end, when the father miraculously recovers from his war-induced amnesia and runs out after his daughter who is being dragged away, shouting her name in the pouring rain, Emily had cried so hard that her teacher, Mrs. Everett, had to take her out into the hall so that the rest of the class could finish the movie undisturbed. Mrs. Everett knew by that point that family was a touchy subject for Emily and probably regretted the choice of film that year. As she tried to console her, Emily had sobbed "take me home; take me home" against the teacher's stomach. Mrs. Everett soon called Lucy to come get her daughter early, not understanding whose "home" Emily had been crying for. Not the place she lived with her mother and her mother's boyfriends, the revolving door of dull and/or deadbeat men throughout most of Emily's childhood. Until Dwayne showed up. Then the revolving door, as well as the relative peace and stability of Emily's earliest years, ceased altogether.

Lucy got back in the car minutes later. The visit had been much shorter than usual.

"Everything okay?" Emily asked.

Lucy buckled her seatbelt right away but did not start the engine.

"He was getting ready to go to the beach. He's got that new caretaker now. Lady from Boston, comes almost every day, even most weekends as far as I can tell."

"Cozy for Dwayne," Emily said. Her mother looked at her briefly then directed her eyes back to the front of the house.

"He likes her," Lucy continued.

"Sounds like it," Emily said absently, digging into her phone.

Her mother didn't say anything for almost a minute. "Real heavy Boston accent. Y'know." She tried to pull off the park-the-car-at-Harvard-yard shtick but failed miserably.

"That was great Mom," Emily deadpanned. "What was that? Jamaican?"

"Shut up," Lucy said, looking up at the gray sky. "He really wants to go to the beach."

"In this weather?"

Lucy shrugged. "It's the wind, I guess. He can't swim, at least not without tons of assistance. But he flies kites. That's what he likes to do all day long, whenever there's enough wind. He likes to be on the beach, the grayer the better probably, fewer people around. Watching those kites soar."

Lucy leaned the side of her head against the window and began tapping the glass lightly with her knuckles.

Emily mindlessly thumbed through texts, jabbing at the screen as hard as she could.

"Are you jealous?" she said eventually, as quietly as she could. Lucy reached over and knocked the phone out of her hands. It clattered down between Emily's feet.

"Mom, the fuck!" Emily yelled.

Lucy didn't say anything, only bent her fingers around the steering wheel and closed her eyes.

Moments passed.

"It's not right," Lucy said, still gripping the wheel.

"What's not?" Emily asked.

"What happened to him? Young and strong as he was. Right in his prime."

"Shit happens, doesn't it?" Emily said.

"What the hell is the matter with you?"

"Mom..."

"I know the two of you didn't see eye to eye—"

"Mom!!"

The inside of the car fell silent.

"If you want me to keep coming with you," Emily began.

"I know."

"I have boundaries."

"I know," her mother assured her, "and I respect them, don't I?"

"Do you?"

Lucy looked at Emily but didn't say anything.

"Just not right," she concluded. "Of all the stupid things. After everything he'd been through. The tours in Afghanistan, then Iraq. Seeing the things he saw. Doing the things he had to do. To go through all of that, make it out alive and in one piece, then to fall off a goddamn stupid ladder." Lucy took a tissue from her pocket and dabbed her eyes. Emily picked up her phone and pocketed it in her sweatshirt. "Somehow," Lucy continued, "that gets me more than anything. When I think about those wars. All that waste; all that death. But somehow, it doesn't get to me the same way. Or it gets me in here"—she pointed to her head—"but not in here"—then to her heart. "But when I think about Dwayne. When I see him like that..." Lucy turned and looked out the window. Her daughter could feel texts piling up and was eager to check them. Her mother soon faced forward again but she didn't say anything more. Emily checked her messages.

Soon the caretaker from Boston came outside and crossed the front lawn. She seemed to be headed to her car which was parked on the street, though Emily wouldn't be surprised if she was covertly surveying the holdup in the driveway. She had short, curly dark hair and lots of freckles. She looked to be about Lucy's age, somewhere in her mid-forties. The Boston woman waved at the two in the car as they fidgeted and held up their hands in return. Emily looked ahead at the front door of the house as it swung open. She caught sight of Dwayne parked in the foyer. Emily couldn't tell whether he was looking at her the way she was looking at him, but she suspected that he was. He had gained weight, she could tell, especially around the neck, and his hair had thinned significantly. His arms were bigger too. It appeared for a moment as though he might come out onto the stoop. His wheels inched slightly forward then rolled back again. Lucy leaned forward, her chin almost touching the wheel, perhaps expectantly. Then Dwayne rolled back, away from the doorframe and deeper into the shadows of the living room. *Did I do that?* Emily asked herself. *Did I push him back?*

The caretaker passed them again, gave another large, exaggerated wave, then marched back up the steps and into the house, shutting the door behind her. Dwayne was gone from sight once more. Emily had only a rough idea of what he looked like now. Appropriate, she thought, since theirs had been a relationship more of sound than of sight. The sound of empty glass bottles clanking in the garbage can. The sound of his belt cracking. The sound (and smell) of his voice in her face telling her to keep quiet or else he'd really give her something to cry about. The sound of her fingers cracking beneath the heel of his boot. Then soon after, and so much worse, the sound of Lucy scolding her daughter for somehow getting her fingers "jammed in the door" so that Lucy had to take her daughter "yet again!" to the emergency room. Then, the sound that had made all the difference in all three of their lives. The wooden rung snapping at the very top of the ladder. Followed by Dwayne toppling down from where he had been cleaning the gutters. Finishing with a second snap: that of his neck and a portion of his spine. The one sound Emily hadn't heard, the only one she wished she had.

Did I push him back? Emily again wondered. *Does he know deep down that it was me?*

"Are you ready?" her mother asked.

"I'm ready," Emily answered immediately.

Lucy started the engine.

"Let's go to the movies."

———————

Emily remembered how difficult it used to be to find parking at the Multiplex on Saturday nights. Now there was space everywhere, it seemed. The back lot was nearly empty.

They parked beneath the sign next to the highway advertising the current roster of movies.

"Anything look good?" Emily asked, studying the sign.

"How about the one about the zoo?" her mother suggested.

"Oh. Isn't it for kids?" Emily asked.

Lucy shrugged. "It looks happy." She paused. "What? Don't kids who take AP classes like to laugh just like everyone else?"

"No, we're too busy extracting then reinserting pointy steel objects up our asses," Emily replied dryly, then followed with, "Sure, we can see the zoo movie."

"That's good," Lucy said. "Let's see the goddamn zoo movie."

Emily stood next to the posters while her mother used the bathroom. She still didn't know why they were here, of all places. What did her mother want her to know? Did it have something to do with Dwayne?

"Anything look good?" her mother asked when she came back out.

Emily shook her head. "Nothing for me."

Lucy rolled her eyes. "Will never as long as I live understand what you have against the movies. What's not to love?"

The usher tore their tickets. They passed by the self-serve candy station.

"Pralines?" Lucy asked.

"Gummy peaches," Emily countered.

"Chocolate almonds," her mother suggested.

Emily nodded. Done deal.

They settled closer to the screen than Emily would have liked to sit, but she didn't complain. She sensed that her mother's comfort was the priority. Her vision wasn't great these days and she was still too proud to wear glasses and couldn't stand the thought of poking contact lenses into her eyes.

It was a nice enough film. Wholly unremarkable, but also slightly exceeding Emily's expectations. Lucy and Emily sat through the credits and the feel-good music at the end. The lights came up. Everyone else left. The ushers came in to sweep the ground.

"Did you like it?" Emily asked.

"Yeah," Lucy said. Moments passed. "Did you hear about the guy who was shot?"

"Shot where?"

"In a movie theatre," Lucy said. "He was texting his daughter's babysitter or something, and some other guy got angry about something, and, well I don't know the ins and outs, but the guy with the phone ended up getting shot in the chest. Died there in his seat."

"Around here?" Emily asked.

"I think maybe in Texas," Lucy said.

"Figures."

"How so?"

"Some of the loosest gun laws in the country."

Lucy regarded her then. "You're not one of those, are you?" she asked.

"One of what?" Emily said.

Lucy didn't reply and the two looked up at the empty screen in silence.

"Could happen anywhere, I suppose," Lucy said eventually.

"Where have you been?" Emily asked.

Her mother regarded her. "What do you mean?"

"There have been, like, countless shootings in the past year alone. So much bigger, and worse, than the one you're talking about."

Lucy faced forward. "You're right. That one just stuck with me. Not sure why." She thought for a moment. "Nobody talks to each other anymore. Nobody just disagrees. People should be able to dislike each other in peace, without getting killed for it." Moments passed. "It's just too much," she said quietly, her eyes on the screen. "Movies try to make it all smaller, I think, try to contain it, but it spills out anyway. The ugliness. The hate." Lucy took a deep breath. "All the ugliness and hate between people in this world. I used to think I could at least try to keep it out of my own household, but it crept in anyway. Didn't it?"

They sat in silence again, each waiting for the other to take the conversation further, either away from the cliff or over it. Each waiting, perhaps, for the other to confess.

"Wanna see another?" Emily asked instead. "A double feature?"

"I'd like that," Lucy said right away.

———

The next film was a mindless thrill ride of crashing helicopters, narrow escapes out of collapsing tunnels, remarkably gradual explosion sequences, slow-motion stunts, hot babes, speedboats flipping through the air, buildings erupting in flames. Guns. Guns. Guns. Guns.

Lucy loved every second, laughing out loud even at parts that weren't supposed to be funny.

"That rocked!" she shouted during the credits. Emily was about to suggest that they go get something to eat at the diner, but Lucy turned to her suddenly with wide, excited eyes.

"I think we might still be able to see the shark movie!" She clutched Emily's arm. "Maybe we can even"—she looked around quickly then whispered—"sneak in this time."

"You wanna see the movie about the giant sharks?" Emily asked.

"I wanna see the movie about those giant fucking sharks," her mother replied.

———

Halfway through the blockbuster sci-fi action movie about giant ge-netically-enhanced sharks, the third and final flick of the evening, Emily got up from her seat, scooted past her mother, walked up the aisle and out of the theatre. She crossed the maroon-carpeted hallway and exited through the heavy double doors. She looked for something to wedge beneath it so that she wouldn't get locked out. Then, finding nothing within reach, she stepped out of her right shoe and shoved it between the door and the frame to keep it from closing. It was chilly out and she could feel the coldness of the sidewalk through her sock. She shifted her weight to her other foot and held her arms tight to her chest. The breeze prickled her skin, drawing goosebumps. She rubbed them hard then dropped and swung her arms around and around. The rear parking lot was as empty as it had been hours before, perhaps emptier. She closed her eyes and tried to clear her mind so that it was as empty as the lot before her. When she opened her eyes again, she realized then what it was she hated about the movies. People gathered together for what seemed to her to be a stupid reason—chosen help-lessness. So many people were determined to sit and receive. Her adult life was lying just ahead of her, ready to be undertaken, and she would not—*not*—be a passive spectator in it. No. She would be agent rather than audience. She had decided that long ago. She had decided that before she had sawed the edge of the rung. But cutting that wood had been like signing a contract with her own soul. The rung became a corner piece of her renewal, a prop, a pillar. But she hated it. She hated what she had done, and she hated even more that she'd do it again if she had to.

"You made this," Emily suddenly said to the parking lot, to every-thing that was not there, and to the nothing that was. "You made this violence. I did not make it, I only remade it. But the violence was there, and I never asked for it. This violence is yours, but I cannot disavow it. It belongs to me now too. And if you try to stop me, if you try to bring it all down, if you try to sever the rungs out from under me, you better believe I'm still gonna climb. I'm going to make it to that top. Blade in hand."

Emily took a deep breath, turned away from the parking lot, put her shoe back on, and let the emergency exit swing slowly shut behind her.

———————

When she sat down again, she looked at her mother and saw that Lucy's eyes were closed.

"Mom," Emily said gently. Her mother opened her eyes and looked at her dreamily. She smiled softly then turned and looked back up at the screen. She wasn't worried, Emily knew. Her mother may not have even realized she was gone.

Emily slumped down in her seat and checked her phone. The movie should be over soon. The last battle sequence appeared to be under-way. Man v. mutant shark. The hero was getting ready to detonate an explosive inside the shark's body. When he blew the monster to smithereens tons and tons of blood as well as a dismembered fin sank down into the depths. Humanity saved again. She looked over at her mother whose eyes were half-lidded. *She's about had it*, Emily thought. She looked up at the screen again. And then, all of a sudden, Emily understood. She looked at the side of Lucy's face. *No*, she thought. *No, no, no, please don't let it be so*. But she knew that it was. It had to be. She knew why her mother had brought her here. She knew why she was afraid to stay but even more afraid to leave. She knew why the inevitable silence between them was infinitely more terrifying than anything the big screen had to offer. Because in that silence was the truth: it had come back. The doctor's visits. The stomach pains. The pills. How could Emily have missed it? Why hadn't she asked? How could it not have occurred to her until now? Because they'd both developed blind spots, she realized. The tight, intuitive bond they'd once shared had long been severed, and only splinters of insight remained. And it would be worse this time, she could sense. The roots of the cancer were deep. They would likely be inoperable. It was only a matter of time. No. Perhaps not of time. Maybe only a matter of space.

Her mother turned to her as soon as the credits began to roll. "Let's go," she said and stood up. Emily nodded and quietly followed.

When they emerged into the lobby, the glass case containing dunes of yellow popcorn was dark. The soda machines were shut down. Everyone was sweeping and locking doors and registers. The vintage neon signs near the ceiling were switched off. There was one door left standing open and it was waiting for the few remaining customers, waiting for them. As soon as Emily stepped out onto the sidewalk, she turned and looked back in at the darkening building. Its unplugged signs and posters were like the adornments of an ancient temple being stripped away as its custodians prepared for the sad inevitability of its consignment to the ages. She would miss hating it, Emily realized. And she would absolutely hate missing it.

"How are you feeling?" Emily asked after they climbed back into the car.

Lucy turned and gave the same soft, tired smile she had given in the theatre.

"Pretty wiped."

"Are you hungry?"

Lucy looked forward then shook her head. "Think the snacks took care of me. You?"

Emily thought about it for a moment then shook her head as well.

"You okay?" her mother asked.

"Yeah," Emily said quickly.

"You don't have to come with me anymore if you don't want. To see Dwayne," Lucy said.

"Okay," Emily said.

Moments passed.

Emily turned on the radio. Dylan was on Brookdale Public Radio. "Lay Lady Lay."

Emily thought briefly about searching for something else, something lighter, but then she sat back, allowing the music to fill the car like warm water.

They sat there looking through the windshield as cars drove past along the highway.

"Emily," Lucy said eventually.

Emily turned and looked at her. "What is it, Mom?"

Lucy was staring at her lap. "Are you...?" she started to say in a small voice, almost like a child's. "Are you still angry at me?" Emily didn't reply and her mother couldn't bring herself to look up at her. "You probably never stopped, right? And why would you? Stop hating me, that is."

Emily kept her eyes forward. She had rehearsed this scene so many times. Had the script memorized. Emily turned to her mother and took a deep breath.

"No," Emily replied, surprising them both. "No, I'm not. Not anymore."

Lucy nodded and looked again at her lap. Emily could tell she was trying not to cry.

There will be fear ahead of us, Emily knew. There will be degradation and agony and rot. And some of that rot will be the things left unsaid, the wrongs unavenged, the sins never entirely absolved. There were some things that might still one day be, and others that now only were. There was the darkened theatre behind, the cars passing by up ahead, and the soft blue light coming from the stereo and the low music and necessary silences therein. Music that sounded to Emily, then, like forgiveness.

"Ready?" Lucy asked after enough time had passed.

"Yeah," Emily replied.

Lucy started the car and turned onto Route 35 heading south.

Emily watched it roll past like a series of still frames stretched out before her: its banks, its chain restaurants, its retail outlets, its supermarkets, its bars, its bowling alleys, its sport shops, its custom designer depots, its oil puddled alleyways, its fat red bubble letters, its papery patches of frayed earth, its deep sunk houses, its roaming teenagers, its cycling workers, its wasting enterprises, its closed delis, its neon heyday, its final lights.

WHAT THE STATUE THINKS

L eonie insists that the stone owl is still out there somewhere on the Upper West Side. When her mother lived there back in the eighties, there had been such an ornament perched on the fire escape outside her apartment. The owl had been there when she moved in. Neither she nor her roommates had even thought about taking it down, in part out of fascination and in part out of fear. The random totems of the city could, after all, be demigods in disguise, prepared to bestow alms for young actors if honored, or ruined careers if offended. When Leonie's mother told her about her life as an aspiring actress in New York, the owl always came to Leonie's mind. She thought of it as a protective spirit overseeing her mother's young and ambitious life, a floating benevolence amidst an otherwise harsh and deeply indifferent landscape, one that Leonie very much needed now in her own life. When Leonie walks around the neighborhood early in the morning or late at night after a party or a show or a late shift at the restaurant, she always keeps an eye out for the stone owl in the neighborhood where her mother had once lived, close to where Leonie is now subletting from a friend. But to date, she hasn't found it, which likely means that it is gone. It doesn't stop her, though, from looking. And New York City is a place where a person never grows weary of looking up.

Leonie knows it won't last much longer. Her friend will return from her West End run at the end of the month, and Leonie will need to relocate once more. Possibly back out to Brooklyn or uptown, she hasn't made up her mind. There are times when she thinks about getting out altogether, times when the forbidding, dispiriting costs of absolutely every single thing feel overwhelming and oppressive. And though she'd notched a few national commercials and had supporting roles in several Off-Broadway plays under her belt, it still feels at times like she is rubbing sticks together as fast as she can, but no matter how hard she works, the spark simply won't catch. This had been fine, certainly, at 23 and 26 and even 29 and then 30. But as she is now rounding the corner toward her 35th year on this earth, the question can no longer be quickly or easily ignored: is this going anywhere? Am *I* going anywhere? "Yes or no," she sometimes begs of the universe. "Just please, tell me one way or the other, once and for all. Yes. Or no?"

Her mother had known when to quit. She had been in her mid-30s when she met Leonie's father, who at the time was in training at what was then Mount Sinai St. Luke's Hospital. She had been playing Ruth Younger in *A Raisin in the Sun*, not knowing her future husband was in the audience. There with a date who had dragged him to the theatre (and likely regretted doing so), he had become mesmerized instead by the woman onstage. Leonie's father had wanted to go into private practice near his hometown in central Jersey, and Leonie's mother, who had by then developed the same love-hate relationship with the city that Leonie is now experiencing, had felt that the time was right to focus on raising a family. Her acting work had started to dry up, and the roles she was being offered—the relatively few that existed for Black women at that time—started to feel more and more degrading. Still, Leonie often wonders if her mother regrets her decision. Was it too soon? Isn't any acting worth it, even acting in bad roles? What if she had hung in there longer?

She has always struggled to get a read on how her mother actually feels about Leonie now following in her footsteps. The support is always unconditional, generally free of the hand-wringing so common among the parents of actors, but there is also a muteness on the subject, a slight drag on the tempo of interest, a tendency toward long pauses when Leonie explains what she's rehearsing or auditioning for. Her mother smiles and nods but usually avoids follow-up questions and is always quick to affirm that Leonie will find success "no matter what she does." Sometimes her mother sighs through her nostrils, other times she narrows her eyes to the ground. Leonie knows that there are still wounds in her mother's heart that have never fully healed: ideas of who she was that had been forged in the blazing fire of a child's mind that had been shattered, savagely and sorrowfully, on the unforgiving shores of the dream indefinitely deferred. Leonie wants to tell her that things are different now, that there are more opportunities than before. But part of her knows that this would only hurt her mother more. And so, what should bring them closer together drives them further apart. *Does she want me to succeed or have to compromise like she did*? Leonie wonders. *Would my breaking through be too hard for her? Would it raise too many what-ifs?* These are the kinds of questions Leonie asks herself as she returns to her apartment after work, on her way to share some late-night Indian food with Samson who will surely be waiting up to hear about her day. (The more he hears about her life, the less he has to think about his own.) Leonie takes the long way home, as always, roaming around the Upper West Side in search of an owl that is either still out there somewhere or else took flight long ago.

Samson decides not to go back up to the apartment just yet after getting his coffee and muffin from the corner deli. He does not want to risk waking Leonie, who has an audition later on. Samson has his notebook with him as he walks to Central Park to see if anything will come to him this morning. He passes The Dakota and crosses Central Park West, passing the "Imagine" mural where even now, this early, someone is on a park bench strumming a guitar and flowers have been arranged at one of the two sites of perpetual mourning in the city.

He leaves Strawberry Fields and makes his way to the Lake. He turns off before Bethesda Terrace and finds a place to sit. There is a light mist over the water, and the city's various utterances, from car horns to the plodding of morning joggers, seem much more distant than they actually are. A person could delude themselves into thinking that they were someplace far away if they were strategic and dedicated enough to the illusion. Samson wonders what it would take to inhabit the park indefinitely. Probably too difficult nowadays. They've sanitized and secured it so much. Could a person get away with camping out in The Ramble or North Woods, subsisting off whatever they could scavenge? Doubtful. Then again, disappearing acts were everywhere. The homeless did it every day. The world's most underrated magicians.

Samson opens his notebook and makes notes. He lists what he's encountered so far: "Imagine. Water. Invisible." He crosses out the last and circles the first. He enjoys staying at Leonie's place, so close to the park and the ghosts surrounding it. He likes to fantasize about moving in step with those ghosts, retracing the path John and Yoko walked once upon a time. He regrets that Café La Fortuna is no longer there. He would love to sit with Leonie out back on the patio, where the photo was taken of Yoko lighting a cigarette and Lennon resting his chin on his hand, staring off. *I am as old now as he was when he died*, Samson realizes. "Life begins at 40," he once heard, and wonders whether it's true or whether that's something only the dead can know.

He looks back at his notebook and scribbles out "Invisible" entirely. He looks at the second word, "Water." He thinks about Jacob, who would still be sleeping back in Colorado. He will have swimming lessons later on today. Samson's wife, Becca, will be there with him, even though it was supposed to be an opportunity for him to bond with his son. Samson tears out the page and crumples it up. The nearest trash can is several yards away. He lets the ball roll to the ground then feels immediately guilty, stands, and throws it away. He closes his notebook. Nothing more, he decides. Nothing more right now.

———————

Her audition is in half an hour and Leonie is starving. She thought the Superfood Smoothie that Samson had left in the refrigerator from yesterday—consisting of protein powder, almond milk, frozen blueberries, spinach, flaxseed, and black pepper—would be enough to get her through the morning. It most definitely was not. Not by a long shot. She steps into a bodega and orders a bacon, egg, and cheese bagel. She takes it without ketchup and tells herself that that equals cutting calories. She finds a place to sit, unwraps her sandwich, and digs in. There is another woman, several years younger than Leonie, sitting on the bench next to her. Leonie thinks she's seen her before at an audition and has a feeling that they will both be trying out for the same part. It's the lead in a new play about a mother and daughter living upstate. They receive a package that turns out to be the cremated remains of the young woman's father, who died of a heart attack while having an affair at a local motel. The mother and daughter spend most of the play arguing about what to do with the remains, what to do with their past. The character Leonie is auditioning for is well-drawn and would give her a lot to work with. She is just on the cusp of being too old, she knows, but she has played similar parts in the past.

As she bites into her sandwich, Leonie glances at the other woman's laptop and can see her working on her website, which contains multiple headshots and videos. The woman looks over at her and smiles. Leonie smiles back, the sandwich still half in her mouth and a blob of cheese dripping out from the other end onto the tin foil. She can't help but hate herself a little just then. She looks forward and asks herself, as she has many times before, why she can't get it together to create a damn website. Not having one feels like being invisible. Leonie hates this. She hates it because what she has always loved about acting most of all—and why she knows she is so good at it—is the fact that you can get into a role so completely that you as a person, an identity, dissolve entirely. The actors she has always treasured the most are able to do just that: disappear, almost without a trace. But the culture today demands loud and clear declarations: This Is Me—I Am Here—I Know What I Want—I Know What I Am—End Discussion. Authenticity has won the day against artifice. Now, actors are expected to hold still. To be consistently and unmistakably themselves, and to build that self into something you needed to watch. Content you couldn't turn away from. Something that would hardly change or falter. Something that was both genuine and edgy. Something that said only what it meant and meant only that. Something frozen yet compulsively knowable. Maybe she had misread the culture. Maybe there still was a niche for the kind of artist Leonie knows herself to be, and maybe that niche is big enough to keep her going. Maybe she can be herself, which happens to mean getting as far away from that self as she possibly can, and still be successful, website or not. Maybe. But Leonie also knows that the woman on the bench next to her is younger and prettier and is more likely to get the part than she is. She seems to know it too and smiles and waves at Leonie as she packs her things and gets up to go to the audition. Leonie smiles through the last, large mouthful. And yes, she still hates herself a little, just a little, just enough to work even harder to become someone—anyone—else.

———————

Samson tries and fails all afternoon to leave the park. Instead, he has taken short naps on both Sheep Meadow and the Great Lawn. He has wandered through Shakespeare Garden. He has spent a long time on the deck of Belvedere Castle, watching the turtles bobbing below. He has received a number of texts from Leonie. Her audition went well. The director has invited her to a party tonight up in Inwood. When he didn't reply, she asked if everything was okay. He answered with a simple, "Yeah, have fun!" followed by a heart emoji which seemed to be enough to keep her from asking more. When Becca calls, Samson is watching ducks land in the Reservoir. He briefly considers throwing his phone in the water with them.

"Hi," he says at the last second.

"Now okay?" she asks.

"Sure," he says, turning away from the water and heading down-town.

"I haven't heard from you in a while," she says.

"Been busy," he lies.

"With her?" Becca accuses. Samson doesn't respond. "Poor thing," she says. "Lisa?"

"Leonie," he corrects. He guesses that his wife doesn't actually care.

"Do you love her?"

"Becca..."

"Do you?"

"Can't it wait?"

"What, Samson? Oh, should we make small talk first? Okay, fine. Let's make small talk. So, let's see. What's new? Well, for starters, the dean *and* the head of the English department keep calling. Sometimes they take turns—it almost feels like phone-tag, you're it, now you're it!—and sometimes they call together. Conference call. The amazing thing is that they call *me* to ask when you'll be back to work, not you. They never call you. Why is that?"

"You know why that is," Samson says.

"Because they don't have your number. How convenient for you. So, what should I tell them, Samson? Can you at least tell me that?"

"Tell them the truth."

"That you don't know."

"That I don't know," Samson confirms.

"And when do you expect you'll know."

He doesn't respond.

"If it weren't for your novel," she continues. "Thank God you got that thing published when you did. I can't imagine any other employer putting up with this. You must really have some clout there. Or else you have something on someone. Have you blackmailed any of the other faculty?"

"That's not a real question, right?"

Becca pauses. Joggers pass in both directions and a horse carriage trundles languorously past.

"When are you coming home, Samson?" she finally asks.

"I don't know," Samson replies honestly.

"Because you're in love with her?" she says, her voice flat.

"I think so."

"Is it only that?"

"I don't know."

"Are you still in love with me?"

Samson keeps walking and doesn't know what to say. If he could find the words, he would tell his wife that based on the little he understands about his or anyone's heart, he is now persuaded that the heart is not stationary, that it drifts and migrates, that it not only beats but also divides like the body's cells. That it is a permanently restless thing that absorbs far more than it can replenish, that deprives far more than it can hope to redeem. Instead of this, though, Samson says simply, "Yes, Becca. I am."

"Then why is this happening?" she asks, on the brink and at a loss. "If it was just a fling, an affair with some hot actress you met at some stupid goddamn reading you gave in the city, we wouldn't be okay. We might not make it back out. But at least I'd know what was happening. I'd have a grip. But this. I don't know what this is!"

"I'm trying to figure it out," Samson says. "Please believe me, Becca, I'm trying—"

"Well, try fucking harder, you asshole!" she yells then tries to control herself, probably for Jacob's sake in the other room. "Try harder," she rasps into the phone, her teeth clenched the way they do when she is fundamentally, inconsolably shaken. "Try harder because you're killing me. You hear me. You're killing me—you're killing *us*!"

Samson abruptly stops and turns, encroaching into the jogger's lane. A woman nearly barges into him, then gives him a long dirty look as she arcs exaggeratedly, making sure to squint with cold and lingering disdain long after rounding his obstruction. "Is he...?"

"Is he what, Samson?"

Samson does and doesn't know what he wants to ask.

"He misses you," Becca says, preemptively, her voice mellowing slightly.

"Does he ask?"

"Every day. What do you expect?" She pauses, then, "He loves you, Samson."

Samson's face begins to crunch. He takes a breath and straightens up.

"Tell him..." he begins.

"Samson..."

"Tell him I..."

"I know. I do," she confirms.

Tell him it's hard, Samson wants to say. Tell him what he can't articulate yet but likely has already begun to intuit in the way children do. That life is something beyond most of us. That it exacts prices at every turn and offers little in the way of clarity or compensation. That it chisels off one piece and then the next, usually when you have no idea what's happening or why. Tell him that his daddy feels most days like a failure. A sliver of what he was meant to be, trapped in the shadow of what he had erected in his mind long ago. And now it has crashed down and covered him like rubble, and he's pushing his hands up through the rock and mortar, but above each and every rock he pushes past there is another and then another and the pushing is becoming heavier than the rocks themselves. And so, he has stalled for the moment. He has ceased to climb and considers it preferable to sinking back down. Tell him his daddy holds him in a place, though, that no stone or rock or even boulder can crush. Tell him that he is for me what I could never amount to in my own heart. Something solid and unyielding. Something that will withstand the erosion of years and setback. Tell him that he is more in my life than I might be able to be in his. Tell him. Tell him. Tell him, please.

"I have to go," Samson says suddenly.

"Wait," Becca says.

"I'll call you. It will get better soon. I'll call."

"Samson, please, please—"

Samson hangs up.

Becca does not try calling again nor does he expect her to. He keeps walking. Past the fountain, the meadow. Past the carousel and the playgrounds. He emerges, at last, at the southwest corner. He crosses to Columbus Circle and stands at the base of the statue. When his parents brought him to the park as a child, he'd look up at the statues on their gigantic pedestals and wonder what they were thinking. They had eyes after all. If they had faces and eyes, then surely there must be something going on behind them. He would close his own eyes and try to put himself in the minds of the statues. He knew rationally that they thought nothing. But he couldn't fathom what nothing actually meant. He imagined it as a word. The word "nothing" flashing behind their still eyes in large lightning letters. But of course, that would be something. Pure nothing was inconceivable, and imagining the world through the eyes of statues was an exercise in both creativity and torment.

Samson looks up at the statue now, surveying a city and beyond it a country that was becoming less and less willing to pay it tribute. Like an idol wasting away beyond the walls of an abandoned fortress, silently demanding homage from a civilization that has determined that the only way to achieve its future is to refuse its past. He closes his eyes and tries once more to see the world through the eyes of nothing. And upon finally conceding that he will never, so long as he lives, fully conceive of what the statue thinks, Samson sits on the lowest step and watches the streetlights along the fork of Broadway and Central Park West sizzle from red to green in their long unbroken chain of lights.

———————

Leonie is at the party and starting to feel tired, the way she often does at parties, but she tries not to show it. People usually see her exhaustion, though, and sometimes it embarrasses her. She doesn't know what it is exactly. Maybe the steady din of people's voices sliding around in crowded rooms, the hypnotic lull of people talking for the sake of talking. The lonely laughter. Or the fact that, in some ways, parties feel more like auditions than auditions do. Having to shake yourself out in front of others. Cultivate the right impressions; seize the right moments. Yes, it is all so very necessary, and it makes Leonie so very tired. And if she drinks much, or if she smokes something, then she is down for the count in a matter of minutes. So, on this particular occasion she avoids both and tries to stay alert because, this time, she is gunning for it. She is prepared to go all in. She plays the game as best she can: she chats and brags and listens and laughs and charms. And within the hour she is out on the fire escape by herself smoking a joint and checking her phone.

Leonie starts writing the texts to Samson that she has tried to write for days, weeks. "How much longer can we...?" Delete. "I think it would be best if you..." Delete. "What exactly are...?" Delete.

In the kitchen, a group of fellow artists is talking politics. They've all attended a march or a demonstration somewhere in the city over the weekend and are planning to attend more this week. They're talking about changing the system, upending it if necessary. Leonie leans her head against the brick wall and listens and smokes and sighs. She doesn't know how to enter these conversations, so it seems best to stay outside. Every time such things come up, she falls back into the swimming pool.

When Leonie was ten years old, she met the cousin of one of her closest friends who had been visiting from Tennessee, a girl named Samantha. The girls went in a group to the beach club where Leonie's family belonged. Leonie and Samantha had chatted pleasantly for most of the afternoon, having things in common that the other girls didn't, such as their ardent devotion to Backstreet Boys as opposed to those posers NSYNC. Then, at the club, once they had their suits on, the girls all made a line and ran together to jump in at the deep end. But when they got to the concrete lip of the pool, Samantha's hand jerked from Leonie's and she stopped abruptly at the edge, as though she had collided into a wall. The other girls buoyed up and called for Samantha to join them. She gave a bashful smile and shrugged her shoulder to her ear without saying anything, then turned her eyes to her toes. The other girls eventually gave up and splashed their way to the other end of the pool to begin a round of Marco Polo. Samantha stayed where she was, not moving backward or forward, as though trapped between two hard surfaces no one else could see. Eventually, her cousin came up behind her, then pushed Samantha into the pool. Samantha shrieked before hitting the water. She popped up right away and swam as fast as she could to the other end, as far as possible from Leonie.

Samantha stayed at the shallow end, her back pressed against the wall. Leonie paddled over, but as she drew closer, she could see Samantha stiffen and press her back harder against the side. Leonie stopped and floated several yards away, a distance that appeared not to provoke any additional distress. The two looked at each other for a long time, neither knowing what to say. Eventually, Leonie started reporting random facts about her favorite Backstreet Boy—AJ, the bad boy, the troubled one—anything that came to her mind, true or not. After a while, the look on Samantha's face began to change, and her body relaxed, and they began chatting almost as easily as they had before arriving at the club. And so, they reestablished their connection across a distance of several yards in chlorinated water, but the distance had been necessary. And it had cost them both something. They'd grown older that day, having to concede to forces that neither had conjured but which had controlled them, nonetheless.

The distance. One of the most awesome powers Leonie has ever encountered. Capable of dissembling then reassembling itself in an instant, so that as soon as you think it's vanished it has already matured in a new form, just over there, around the corner, under your feet. The distance. So timeless one had to wonder whether we had made it, or it had made us. Was it outside or within? The shapeshifting distance. The unconquerable distance. The apartness that is America. One felt almost awed by it. One might even be tempted to defer to it on occasion, as you'd behave in a church or a synagogue or a temple, respectful not only of the worshippers but also the worshipped, the ruling figments of the ages, ideas powerful enough to rear and lay waste to entire civilizations. And that's what the distance was, as far as Leonie was concerned. Something permanent, omnipresent. And we could march, and we could create hashtags and memes and change contracts and even a few hearts, and certain things would shift, for a time anyway, but sooner or later they would settle again. And the distance would still be there, obstinate and immutable. Because it had evolved to be just that. Indestructible. *But oh, these aren't good thoughts,* Leonie realizes. These aren't the kinds of thoughts to think at parties like this. These are the thoughts you think when you're sleepy and a little stoned and you know you need to fit in better but have no idea how. These are the thoughts you think when you want to believe that a country can change once and for all, but goddammit you just know better, don't you? You know that the only real way to contend with the distance is to beat it at its own game. And that's what being on stage means. Communicating across a distance between actor and audience that is not so different from the distance in the pool that day. And hope can't be discovered, only created. And time doesn't go backward, but sometimes happiness does. So, we start again, she believes. Each time the lights come up, we create something new and also something old. And we try and reduce the distance. And maybe we give up on change from time to time and learn to hold our ground instead. And we look the distance in the eye and tell it where it ends so that we can begin.

But these are the wrong thoughts at a time and place like this, and so Leonie ducks back into the apartment, wobbly at first then steady on her feet. She meets the director in the kitchen.

"Over it?" he asks.

"What do you mean?"

He nods his head at the party behind him.

"No, I'm good," she says. "Just thinking."

"About what?"

Leonie shrugs. "Different things."

The director nods. "Had that feeling about you."

"What feeling?" she asks.

"That you're deep," he replies.

"I don't know about that," she says.

"I do," the director says. "That's why I thought you were ideal for the role even though the playwright felt otherwise."

"Did he?" Leonie could see the stocky, bearded writer on the other side of the room. She couldn't resist asking, "Who did he like?"

"That Miranda girl, I think," he says. Leonie is pretty sure Miranda is the woman who had been sitting on the bench next to hers before the audition.

"I see," Leonie says.

"Said the blind man," the director jousts.

"What?"

"Never mind."

The music has grown louder in the other room, and the director bows his head and steps closer to whisper something in her ear.

"What would you do?" he asks.

She turns her head slightly to his, their faces mere inches apart.

"What do you mean?" she asks.

"I mean, what would you do? For the part."

Leonie hears the question in one way and responds accordingly.

"I'd do anything."

"Anything?" he follows.

"I'll give my all."

"How so?"

"I'll work my ass off; I'll—"

"What would you do?" he asks again, brusquely this time. "For the role. What would you do?"

Leonie looks at him again. "I..."

She drops her eyes to her feet. *There's the water*, she thinks. *Here I am and there it is. Do I?*

She pushes past him, spilling a cup over the counter in the process. *Fuck these parties*, she thinks. *Fuck these fucking parties*.

Samson lets himself into the building with the spare key Leonie had lent him. He lumbers up the several flights then continues past Leonie's door to the roof entrance. Usually, the door is locked. Tonight, it's not. Samson left his phone somewhere, he's not sure where. He knows Leonie texted him a number of times. He assumes

Becca will call again at some point, maybe once Jacob is asleep. Samson looks out at the glowing giants lining the streets around him, people at work or at play or doing nothing at all behind their windows. *I didn't have what it takes to live here*, he accepts. *I couldn't concentrate. At least, I thought that was the problem. But after I left new struggles emerged. So, it's not the place, is it? I could be here, there, or anywhere. It's me. There's something in me.*

Samson climbs up onto the ledge. He can feel the wind coming off the river. It pushes against him. He widens his arms, soaking the wind. He leans forward, bracing. He drops his arms and opens his eyes. He looks up. He looks down. He looks across. Someone is on their balcony smoking. He can't tell whether she sees him or not. He imagines then that they are looking directly at each other even though neither can locate the other's gaze. He closes, then opens his eyes. Close, open. The wind picks up, then dies down again quickly. He stands as still as he can. He closes his eyes and lifts his left foot up and out over the edge. He lowers it again. Does the same with the other foot. Lift, lower. He alternates back and forth between the two. He wobbles at one point, regains himself and straightens his posture, and recommences his exercise. One foot then the other. Lift, lower. He opens his eyes. The woman is no longer on the balcony. The still figure remains at the edge of the building. The wind picks up.

It is almost daybreak. Leonie considers catching the A train but decides instead to walk. She meanders to the bottom of the hill, then up a path into Fort Tryon Park. She passes The Cloisters and finds a place to sit and look out across the Hudson River as its mists begin to melt away. New Jersey sparkles and winks, and Leonie decides to walk all the way to her apartment. She makes her way through Washington Heights. The city opens its doors as she passes by, news and music in English and Spanish drifting across the sidewalk, the night's shadows fading away. Leonie suddenly feels swept away as though by a current and time dissolves around her and the blocks disappear beneath her, as though she and the streets were moving as one. As she nears Harlem, she begins to run. For no reason. For every reason. Her foot hurts and her back aches but she runs. She is a body awake in the universe and a woman alive in New York City, and so she runs because fuck it. Yes. Dive in at the deep end and feel the cold and love the cold. Have this moment. This one, right now. Don't ask it to be anything more than what it is and don't misjudge it for what it's not. Just have it. This moment. This feeling. This life. Now and now again. Have it. For no reason. For every reason. Have it. Now and now again. Have something of yours even if you'll never have anything of theirs.

As she crosses 110th Street, the clouds eclipse the new sun. Soon after it begins to rain. Leonie takes shelter beneath the green awning of a building and watches as the rain intensifies its heavy-handed assault on the pavement, causing the leaves to twitch and quiver across the street. Leonie crosses her arms against the sudden chill. And then, for no reason in particular or perhaps for every reason there is or ever was, Leonie laughs. *I'm still doing this*, she realizes. Whatever *this* is. Still (sort of) young and still on the doomed trajectory of the life I chose based on the love which chose me. Yes. Come what may or may not, but I'm still here doing it. And maybe the stone owl is out there somewhere, or maybe for the moment it's me. A sign unto myself, high above. And Leonie laughs. She laughs into the rain and into the blazing heart of the city as it sounds its angels around her. She laughs and raises her arms and lets the water burn the ends of her fingers as she lends voice and power to the day.

ACKNOWLEDGEMENTS

Thank you to everyone who has read and responded to the many, many drafts of these stories over the years. Thanks to the forever support of my parents, who have always nurtured the storyteller in me. Thanks to Laine Sutton Johnson and Charles H. Johnson, who read early drafts of the manuscript and gave me reason to believe it was worth pursuing. Thanks to the Writers in Stuttgart for providing so much feedback and wisdom, and for giving me a platform to read a number of these stories to a live audience. Thanks, especially, to Jadi Campbell, whose support has been a true gift. Thanks to Abigail Wild and Wild Ink Publishing for giving my book a home, and to Laura A. Wackwitz, whose insights and suggestions as an editor have been invaluable. Thanks, finally, but foremost, to my son and to my wife, who have always encouraged and inspired me and provided vital feedback that has made these stories so much better. This book is dedicated to everyone who has ever had faith in me and my writing. I hope that you know who you are, and how very grateful I am.

ABOUT THE AUTHOR

Michael Goodwin Hilton is a playwright, poet, and fiction writer. A two-time recipient of the New Jersey Governor's Award in playwriting as well as the Spotlight Award from True Acting Institute, his plays have been produced in festivals across Europe and the United States, and in Manhattan Repertory Theatre, T. Schreiber Studio, and other theatrical venues. He holds degrees from Fordham University, where he studied playwriting and psychology, and the University of Tübingen (M.A. American literature). While a member of a L'Arche community in Ireland, he helped conduct a theatre workshop for adults with intellectual disabilities. He lives with his family in Bavaria, Germany and teaches at the Catholic University of Eichstätt-Ingolstadt. His writing can be found on Substack as well as the New Play Exchange (NPX) and he can be followed on Twitter/X @ AuthorMGH.

What the Statue Thinks merges psychological insights with a theatrical sense of scene to form an unparalleled exploration of the human condition.

Made in the USA
Middletown, DE
19 January 2024